That We Might Have Hope

Season Sinclair

That We Might Have Hope

Manor Home Literary Society • Alabama

Published by Manor Home Literary Society
P.O. Box 381111
Birmingham, AL 35238
Printed in the United States of America

Edited by Truly Wordsworth and Debbie Little.
Illustrations by Abby Little.
Cover photograph and styling by Season Sinclair.

ISBN 978-0-615-99840-4

This book is dedicated to my mother, without whom this book would not be in existence.

Foreword

The American Civil War was a time of struggle and a time of triumph—a match of wills centered on the future of a nation—its economy and character. A time of ladies and gentlemen—an era gone by but forever remembered. The 1800's are brimming with a history that has shaped our nation and continues to warm and grieve our hearts. Great hoop skirts, delicate lace, homemade bread, and gallant soldiers have captured our imaginations of a time forever etched in the halls of our legacy, both North and South. The grief experienced by those who lost much or all that they possessed in this world is beyond what I can describe in these pages. It is true that during the Civil War many a mother lost all of her sons, many a sister lost all the men in her life, and many a home was left vacant. Heroes and heroines have emerged from both truth and fiction from this hallowed time of history. Historians will forever be intrigued by the characters that led the war effort and the battles that left deep scars on the nation.

The pages here contain a story of what might have been, another heroine, making her way in a land stunned by war. A small white farmhouse, a garden, a little town, a doctor and a farmer, and a girl—a girl on the brink of womanhood. While this story takes place in a real time in history, it is fiction, and the characters and places are my creation, created for you to experience what might have been in the 1860's, a world of sorrow and joy and hope and a girl named Kate…

-Season Sinclair

Chapter I

Memories

Kate slid her foot onto the cool wood floor. She pulled back the covers and walked silently to the window where the war-torn landscape lay before her. Her hand trembled as she brushed back loose strands of hair fallen from her braid in the night. The solitary fields spoke to her loneliness. She hung her nightgown on its peg, tied on her petticoat, and slipped her dress over her head. All was silent. Of course it was; there was no one to break it. With each creak of the stairs, a memory flashed before her. She looked down to see her skirt brush past a blood stain on the rough pine floor, evidence that wounded armies had once occupied the home. A shudder rippled through her body. Finally she reached the kitchen, prepared for the cooking she had not been accustomed to doing.

"Anna! You are still here!"

"Miss Kate. You know better than to think that I would just go off and leave you! I aint going nowhere. Not so long as you and I both livin'."

"But Anna, your daughters have gone, and Isaiah and John left yesterday. You do know that you were free to go with them?"

"Course I do! My gals got themselves good husbands to be lookin' out for them, and I aint going nowhere else but right here. Your father built that cabin we live in, and that's where I'm gonna stay."

A ray of sunshine crept into Kate's heart, and she nearly smiled as she patted the woman's arm. Yes, she should have known that Anna would not leave.

"But your husband, what about…" Kate started to ask when Judd came through the kitchen door carrying a fresh load of firewood.

"No, ma'am, I'm not going nowhere. Anna and me, we stayin' right here. Your family been far too good to us for us to leave you 'lone and helpless-like."

"Well, I can do most things; I'm not entirely spoiled," Kate declared.

Nevertheless, she was surprised at the great relief she felt knowing she would not be alone. Before she knew what she was doing, she was holding Anna in a long embrace.

Anna put her hands on Kate's shoulders, "Your breakfast be ready shortly, Miss Katherine. Just busy yourself with somethin' else," she encouraged.

Kate complied, but where would she begin? The house was left tattered and worn from the war.

She walked through the dining room observing the many chairs that circled the table…empty. She continued on to the living area where the furniture also stood empty, its silence seeming to beg for the familiar occupants of the past. Kate glanced down the hallway at the wooden door shut firmly, the lock turned securely. Her parents' room had not been disturbed for many months now, and Kate did not intend to change that. She turned her gaze from the lonely doorway and walked outside to the large front porch. The late spring breeze stirred the curls that hung untended around her face. She leaned heavily against the rail, staring down the lane. In her mind she could see the grey coats on their horses filing past, and the blue coats that had come less friendly. But then, there had been nothing friendly about the war. She passed her hand over her eyes as if to erase those scenes, but she knew it was no use.

Kate's small southern town had endured great turmoil and tragedy, as much of the South had in its Second War for Independence. The boys had left heroically with cheers and tears to protect their homeland and their rights. Many of them had not returned and those left at home had watched and mourned the state of the Confederacy until all hope for victory had been lost. As if it had been yesterday, Kate remembered how she had longed for the end to come. Victory or defeat, the war had lasted far too long and had worn the survivors thin and fragile. The land was bare and lifeless as the farmers had given up the plow for the rifle, and gone to the battlefield. The town had fought in its own way, willingly providing all it could for the Confederate soldiers. Kate's farm was the first on the outskirts of town and though her home was small, it had been ideal for the wounded men. After the end of the war and the last of the wounded had moved out, Kate was no longer kept busy with all the tasks of caring for others. The gruesome pain and suffering had caused a reserve and stoicism to come over Kate. Would life hold hope for the future once more? All she could see was the bleakness of being alone and being constantly reminded of all that had passed. Anna had noticed it and deep within her own heart she was sure she could not leave Kate.

The breeze turned into a gust of wind, and Kate looked toward the sky. Rain in May had excited her father in days passed, as it meant the crops would get off to a hardy beginning. There were no crops this spring, just the small vegetable garden planted earlier in the year that would be enough to feed only a few. Loneliness began to creep in again and she turned back indoors. She went determinedly to the breakfast table where a welcoming meal had been prepared for her.

When she had finished her breakfast, she glanced at the clock. It was not yet nine. A whole day lay before her.

What am I to do? she asked herself. As she walked towards the stairs to retrieve a book from her room, she saw once again the stains on the floor.

She grimaced inwardly. "Those have to go," she said aloud. "Today I'll scrub the floor."

Her book forgotten, she turned towards the water pump, relieved to have something to occupy her. As she entered the kitchen, she saw the row of aprons hanging by the doorway. She chose one suitable for scrubbing and tied it around her.

By midday, Kate had managed to scrub nearly all of the stains on the floor of the farmhouse. They would never be entirely gone, but they were lighter, cleaner.

"Good," she whispered satisfactorily.

Perhaps with Anna and Judd's help, they could do something to restore the charm the farmhouse had once held.

Over the next few months, Kate repaired fences right alongside Judd and worked with Anna to re-paint the shutters. Neighbors helped as much as they could, taking breaks from their own repairs. Everyone had their own catching up to do, and Kate was appreciative of their assistance. Little by little the house took shape. Kate was grateful for the work to keep her busy. The weariness she felt at night overtook her before loneliness could steal her sleep away.

The kitchen garden that had been planted in spring, just after the war ended, was now bringing forth hearty vegetables. Kate would have plenty of food for winter. Inheritance from her father would provide for her for many years to come. Most importantly, she would be able to remain on the farm with her familiar surroundings.

A family photo done just before the war now hung in the hallway. Kate often stopped to observe it: her father bearing his usual kind expression, her older brother Thomas standing just behind her, his hand resting on her shoulder. She could almost feel it there now; he had been so protective and caring. Then there was Caleb next to her, the shy one, but affectionate and loving and attached to Kate. Caleb was the only one who had never known his mother. She had died in childbirth with him, and Thomas and Kate had hardly been old enough to remember her.

Kate would stand there in the hallway and study their faces. Father, Thomas, and Caleb had not returned from the war. A lump would form in her throat and her chest would tighten, but she never cried. Her heart would ache as she had never experienced, and her soul felt as though it would collapse on itself, draining the life from her very being. The silence around her was even worse. It closed in, and without being broken by tears, there was nothing to shake it. She stood thus many times, unable to speak, unable to cry, unable to articulate the great burden of sorrow that she carried deep within her. She would pass on and continue her tasks, possessing the same constant solemn reserve.

It seemed like such a short time ago when she had received that last letter from Thomas. He had sounded optimistic and confident that the Confederacy would prevail. He had also expressed sorrow at not being able to be with Kate as she endured the loss of their father alone. Little did he know that she would soon bear the loss of him as well.

Thom Austin had adored his only daughter and even before his wife's untimely death when Kate was only six years old, he had begun to teach her the particulars of a well-managed farm. Kate returned her father's admiration and could be found close by him at his desk poring over the same books he studied on the lives of great men such as George Washington and Thomas Jefferson. Thom Austin had a great respect for Jefferson and had fashioned his farm and home much like a small Monticello. Montcrest was the name he gave to this land where he worked and raised his family. He had viewed the conflict between the North and South as an unnecessary interruption, and hoped it could be resolved by a peaceful resolution. It was not to be, and so Thom Austin and his sons, looking very gallant in their uniforms, had ridden off to fight for the Confederacy and give their lives for a cause they did not entirely believe in.

Chapter II

Millie

Millie Morgan was Kate's dearest friend and as near to a sister as Kate could have had. Kate could not recall a beginning to their relationship; Millie had simply always been there. The Morgan and Austin farms were adjoining, and the families had enjoyed a close relationship for many years. Millie was a beautiful and poised girl of twenty-two. Liveliness was brought to any gathering simply by Millie's presence, and her smile seemed to permeate wherever she was. Her brother, Conner, had been a close friend to both Thomas and Caleb, and he was almost exactly Thomas' age. He had been like a brother to Kate, and she was glad when he returned from war, though he bore the scars of it like many others. The surgeon had managed to save his leg but with the affirmation that it would never be of much use to him. He refused to believe it. It made Kate shudder to think of the once strong rider he had been, being forced to use crutches forever. However, her heart told her that his determination would not allow it to happen. He had already gone from two to one, and the more he worked and exercised, the more use he regained.

The joy that the Morgan family shared was a treasure and a quandary to Kate, and she often wondered at it. Though the joy of Conner's return was not overshadowed by the grief that they felt for his injury, Kate had still wondered as time went on if perhaps their joy would wane just a bit. But it had not. Not only did Millie continue to possess it, but Conner also wore a smile on his face.

What is it? Kate would ask herself. *What is it that allows them to have such seamless contentment in life?* On the nights that Kate did not drift immediately off to sleep, she lay in bed asking why she herself could not find the peace that the Morgans possessed. Since her own mother's early death, Mrs. Morgan had been as a mother to Kate. She was kind and well respected and loved her two children so tenderly. Kate thought of the many times Mrs. Morgan had made her feel like one of her own. Her conversations would revive Kate's struggling spirits, and without knowing what was taking place, Kate would come to life a bit more. Though Kate was comforted, she never expressed her emotions. They were all internal, and she kept her grief hidden deep within her soul. Oh, it was true that she was kind, serving, caring, and had a loving heart, but her emotions rarely, if ever, surfaced.

Chapter III

Sorrow

Disturbing rumors of a war between the states had culminated into the first battle when Kate was only eighteen years old. As her father and brothers had prepared to join Confederate forces, she had insisted she wanted to remain in her own home with the farmhands and house slaves she had grown up with. Kate assured her father and Thomas that she would be fine there. She would feel more useful, closer to her family, by staying at home. Her father had reluctantly agreed, and Kate had fared quite well. The neighbors looked out for her, and Kate had worked hard to make a difference in the war effort. There were many hands then to assist in the running of the farm and the home. Kate had truly been mistress of the house in her mother's absence since she was very young, and the task of maintaining the home was not as difficult as it might have been for some girls her age. Everyone was concerned when news of the deaths of her father and two brothers reached her in quick succession. Kate withdrew, not willing to come in contact with others. Millie seemed to carry some of the grief as well and had feared even more for her own brother's life.

Now that Kate had come through her grief, or so she thought, she busied herself with making things better. Thanksgiving was fast approaching, and Kate enjoyed baking for the holiday. For Thanksgiving Day she was invited to the Morgans'. Their large farmhouse was filled with holiday comfort, and Kate drew on its reserve, but no matter how hard she tried, she felt herself remain rigid. Mrs. Morgan sensed it, for she sat next to her and remarked on the improvements to Kate's farmhouse. By the end of the day, Kate could not help but feel better, and that night she went to sleep with a good feeling stirring inside.

Christmas came, and she was once again invited to share it with Millie and her family. She left gifts for Anna and Judd who were free to spend the day as they wished. It was only a mile to the Morgans' farm, and Kate enjoyed the walk, even in the brisk, cold December air. The home smelled of fresh baked rolls and pumpkin pie, and a beautiful meal was served. Millie and Conner laughed and talked, and Kate felt at ease. Still no smile filled her once happy face, and her melancholy demeanor did not escape Conner's notice. When the scrumptious dinner feast came to an end, the family and their guest retired to the sitting room. Mrs. Morgan again sat by Kate. The others were busy arranging gifts and making sure everything was in order.

As Mrs. Morgan spoke to Kate in her usual heartwarming way, she assured her that life would hold hope for her once more, that in the approaching new year she wanted to see Kate more often and to visit more often herself. Kate could only nod. She wanted to pour out to Mrs. Morgan the many sleepless nights she had spent—how no matter the warmth of the fire or the comfort of food, the cold absence of humanity permeated her being, and she could not escape it. The downy softness of her bed, the layers of quilts she slept under, the woolen nightgown that clothed her—nothing brought comfort or could warm the cold emptiness of the little farmhouse. But Millie was anxious to open gifts and led Kate to the tree. Kate felt so undeserving of all that she received and was glad that she had put special thought into her gifts for the family.

Once Christmas had passed, the new year came quickly and with it the snowy cold of January. Judd split extra firewood, and they worked together to keep the fires burning. The farmhouse warmed easily. The familiar mugs and teacups were taken more often from the shelf and filled with steaming cider, tea, or cocoa and warmed them in the chilly mornings and late nights. Kate's bedroom was over the kitchen and the heat from the stove below kept her room a little warmer than the other rooms upstairs. She was grateful during the bitter nights.

In front of the fire, the basket by the chair filled with yarn, and Kate knitted a blanket for Sarah Pierce who was soon to become Mrs. Rob Miller. As the blanket took shape, Kate snuggled beneath it, knitting away at the next row. Late one night, Kate felt as though her heart would break from the weight of the silence and loneliness. She took out her sewing box and carefully sorted through her fabric scraps and yarn. She also found in her box a piece of linen that had once belonged to her mother.

"I thought I separated this out from the others," she mourned as she studied the piece. But she ran her fingers over it, imagining how her mother would have used it. A few stitches had been carefully placed as if she had begun

WHATSOEVER

a sampler—a flower and the word "Whatsoever." Kate laid the piece carefully aside.

Kate continued to go to church each Sunday. She sat in the same pew that had once been occupied by four and then three other members of her family, and then finally by only herself. She refused to move, even though the empty places of the pew brought stabbing pain. The Morgans sat behind her. Millie had suggested that they move to be with Kate, but Millie's father thought differently.

"In Kate's mind, those places in that pew rightly belong to someone else. I believe she still sees her brothers and her father there next to her. We can't take that away, not just yet anyway."

Millie had nodded, understanding a tiny bit.

The rest of the town felt as Mr. Morgan did and understood that Kate needed time before filling the seats would not be painful. It was not very often that there were new faces in church. Most everyone there had been there for many years, and so, leaving the seats undisturbed was not an issue.

~~~~~~~~~
~~~~~~~~~

After spending the holidays with the Morgans, Kate thought she had discovered the reason for their joy and their peace. It was their mother. She held things in place. She was kind and compassionate. The home was filled with a sense of security from the competent, loving way in which Mrs. Morgan managed it.

If they ever lost their mother they would lose their joy, she said to herself. *If my mother were here things would be different.*

Mr. Morgan ran the town mercantile and kept the shelves stocked with all the necessary supplies. Kate took her extra eggs in once a week and then applied the egg money to whatever goods she needed to pick up. Mr. Morgan often slipped a licorice stick into the paper bag and Kate would discover it when she arrived home to put away the other things. It had been her favorite candy since she was a child and she had plenty of memories of visiting the store with her brothers and picking candy from the jars that lined the counter. The store was a steady business and blessed the family with an income. The farm had also produced a good crop in the years past, but now with only Martin to work the land, less of the fields were planted. Before the war there were four slaves on the Morgan farm.

They had been rightfully given their freedom and even then had remained for some months before expressing their gratitude and moving on. Martin remained. He had nowhere to go, he said, that would be as pleasant as the Morgan farm.

The vegetable garden, like Kate's, usually produced a hearty yield that fed the family through the winter. Millie had been raised to know the kitchen as Kate had, and she worked alongside her mother. They did not have an "Anna" in the kitchen, but they did have young Jess. She had been orphaned as a little child and Mrs. Morgan had taken her under her wing. When the slaves had gone, she had remained, reluctant to ever leave Mrs. Morgan's care. Jess had insisted on earning her keep and serving her "Missus," as she still called Mrs. Morgan. She kept the farmhouse spotless and hardly a crumb hit the floor before Jess had mopped it up. Conner teased her that she made the best buttermilk biscuits for a hundred miles.

Chapter IV

Aunt Nora

Kate wore her mother's shawl throughout the winter months. She closed her eyes, trying to visualize her mother pulling the shawl lightly around her shoulders. It had been such a long time since Kate was wrapped in her mother's arms, her slender hands stroking Kate's hair, her eyes twinkling as she laughed. Kate desperately needed the memories of her mother's love. She studied the stitches on the quilts she had sewn. The booties she had knitted for Caleb while she awaited his arrival lay in Kate's yarn basket, and she held them. There was one photo of her mother in the house. It sat on the bedside table in her parents' room. So many times Kate had been tempted to retrieve it, but each time as she reached the door and fingered the key in the lock, she drew back, unwilling to open the door to the emptiness. Since her father's death, Kate found herself missing her mother even more.

One afternoon Kate heard a voice outside the door, a woman's voice, talking to Duke, the dog. Kate opened the door and all that was in view was the top of a velvet hat as the woman bent over to pat the dog with her gloved hand. A face turned up under the lace trim of the hat that was tied neatly with a ribbon under her chin.

She stood, revealing a beautiful gown trimmed with frills and pretty buttons. The face was like her mother's, only older, more plump. All of a sudden the woman spoke and broke the trance Kate had fallen into.

"Oh, hello there, my dear. Why, you must be—oh, but surely not." She paused, and Kate remained silent, waiting for her to work out her confusion. "Are you Katherine?"

"Yes, madam, I am Kate." Kate wondered how this woman knew her. It suddenly struck her, *She is one of Mother's friends from long ago and she will have no idea that my family is gone.* Kate became tense, unwilling to have to reveal the events of the past. She led the way into the sitting room.

"Well, Katherine, I hardly expect you to remember me. I am Nora, your poor mother's sister." Kate's eyes widened.

She had heard of Aunt Nora, her aunt from the city, but she had not seen her since she was too young to remember.

"So the men keep to the fields, do they?" Aunt Nora asked, looking around the rest of the house that lay in silence.

"Pity they leave you here alone. And I suppose your father let the slaves go. Yes, he would do something noble like that."

Kate stood silently, unable to speak for Aunt Nora's prattling. She waited until Aunt Nora had removed her gloves, hat, and thick velvet overcoat before she spoke.

"Aunt Nora, I am sorry you did not already know, but I am the only one here now." Kate thought she had communicated sufficiently, but Aunt Nora did not understand. Kate would have to explain—to speak the words *death, died, gone,* and the names of her brothers and her father in the same sentence. All of a sudden she felt dizzy.

"What? They've gone off and left you? Your father after another piece of land and grand endeavor, I suppose. Took both boys with him. Oh, Louise would never have approved..."

Kate finally felt it necessary to interrupt, "Aunt Nora."

"Well, what is it, my dear?"

"My father and brothers were killed in the war." Kate wondered if Aunt Nora would respond in the same abrupt way she had so far. She was surprised when Aunt Nora seemed unable to reply. She simply sank suddenly into the great armchair and said rather forlornly, "I suspected as much, but could not bear to really believe it. I am terribly sorry, Katherine."

Kate sensed true sympathy in her aunt.

"I am sorry that you did not know, Aunt Nora. I did not know to send word to you."

"Nonsense, Katherine. You hardly knew you had an Aunt Nora," she paused. "And I am more sorry than I can say about that. You have had to bear this all alone."

Kate wanted to assure her that she had not been alone, that she had many friends who had supported her, but Aunt Nora spoke again.

"Well, it's just a good thing I came along when I did. You being here all alone is not fitting. You will have to just come home with your Aunt Nora and let me fuss and fret over you."

Kate was horrified, and she must have looked it, for Nora added, "Oh, not immediately; I would like to see this place again for a day or two."

Kate tried to remain calm and fought against the weight of conflict that had come so suddenly to her doorstep. She knew that she should give Aunt Nora credit for being concerned, but beyond that, Kate had no desire to alter her lifestyle and follow a fashionable aunt to the city to be "fussed and fretted" over.

"Aunt Nora, that is very kind. But I have been just fine here."

"Nonsense, girl. Do you not want to get married? You need to be refined and dressed up." Aunt Nora cast a glance over Kate's plain attire. Kate's beauty was evident, clear, and strong, but Kate had never flaunted it. Even in the plain way that she dressed, her beauty was arresting. Those around her were aware of the fact that her outward appearance was enhanced by her great inward virtues. Aunt Nora had lived her life believing that virtue was all about the prim and proper ways of society, as well as an elaborate appearance. Kate shook her head at the thought of being dressed up like the girls in the city.

There was no longer a need to answer as Aunt Nora had already moved on and was inspecting the rest of the house. She moved through each room commenting on its simplicity and its rugged nature, how each window needed a new type of curtain, and how neglected the style had been. Kate sighed. She felt indignation rising at Aunt Nora's comments. The house had been furnished by her parents to be comfortable and useful. The furniture was appropriate for a farmer and his family. Kate reminded herself that Aunt Nora's husband was a wealthy businessman from the city, and Aunt Nora had been accustomed to the fancy things he provided.

Kate finally excused herself to go to the kitchen.

"Kate, what we gonna do? We hardly got enough food to impress ourselves, must less your fancy city aunt!"

"Anna, simply cook the usual; there is no need to impress Aunt Nora. She will just have to understand that this is the way we live and that we are very content that way." Kate's voice was kind but firm, and Anna nodded.

When supper was served, Kate could see on Aunt Nora's face her surprise at the lack of ceremony and at the simple fare before her, but Kate proceeded with her usual reserve. When it came time to show Aunt Nora to a guest room, Kate struggled emotionally. She could not bear the thought of Aunt Nora being the first occupant of her parents' unopened room. Besides, the upstairs room had always been the guest room and it was the one Kate kept ready. She quickly took her gaze from the bedroom door and hastened up the stairs. She desperately hoped that Aunt Nora would not oppose.

To her relief, Aunt Nora followed her without a question. Kate left her there to settle in and returned to the sitting room. She sighed deeply and picked up the hand work that had been cast aside in the flurry of Aunt Nora's arrival. She fingered it, but could not concentrate. "How long will she stay?" She whispered. "How am I to tell her that I must remain here? Or should I—should I go with her…" Her thoughts traveled through the town and she saw the many faces of those she was surrounded by. She could hear the voices as they were raised in song on Sunday mornings and see the faces of the children with their families—she could hear the swaying of the branches and the rustling of the grass, and she knew she could never leave her home. Her father had been a farmer and Kate had been raised to love the things that she was accustomed to having around her. Going to the city might be an adventure for a time, but her heart told her that she would miss her little town far more than she would enjoy Aunt Nora's city.

"I do not believe that she will readily take no for an answer." Kate sighed again. The light in the room was dim, the sun had set, removing its comforting light, and even with Aunt Nora in the house, Kate felt the loneliness enclose around her.

"I wonder what it is that brought her here after all these years," Kate whispered even more softly.

The next day went much the same. Aunt Nora fussed over the draftiness of the house and the small size of the fireplace. However, there were several moments when Kate sensed that Aunt Nora was showing true kindness.

Kate had sent Judd with a message to the Morgans' that she had an unexpected guest and would not be able to make her usual Friday visit but to please come themselves to visit, so she could introduce them to her aunt. Late that afternoon the Morgans' wagon appeared in front of the farm house. Kate welcomed them in and introduced Mrs. Morgan and Millie to Aunt Nora. Anna had put on a clean, starched apron and served tea in the sitting room by a crackling fire that warmed the room nicely. Aunt Nora seemed pleased. Kate noticed the extra doilies set out and caught Anna's eye with a nod of gratefulness. Millie was very kind and asked Aunt Nora all sorts of questions about herself. Kate listened with satisfaction as Millie proved herself to be the kind of friend Aunt Nora would certainly approve of her having.

"Well, Katherine here is going back with me when I return. I daresay you will hardly know her when you see her next, as I am going to see that she is refined in every way." Aunt Nora exclaimed suddenly with a smile as she sipped her tea. Kate looked surprised and Millie gazed on in astonishment.

"Aunt Nora, your offer is very kind, but I cannot leave here. This is my home." Kate spoke evenly and sweetly, at the same time noticing that Aunt Nora always addressed her as "Katherine." Millie look relieved, but it was shock that Aunt Nora expressed.

"Why, Katherine! You will refuse the opportunity to be refined? Your dear mother would be very proud of the connections I could make for you."

Kate's emotions had reached their peak with the last statement and she spoke quickly, "Aunt Nora, with all due respect, the people here are connections that my mother and my father were proud of possessing. These people have loved me and surrounded me during the most difficult of times, and I love them very dearly. We do not need lace and velvet to make matches." Kate's face was flushed, but she spoke evenly. Mrs. Morgan sensed her tension and Millie shifted uneasily.

Aunt Nora lowered her teacup slowly, her eyes wide as she listened to Kate's defense of her town. "You seem quite confident in your decision, and I will not argue." Aunt Nora seemed resolved and satisfied that at least she had attempted and made a good offer.

Finally Mrs. Morgan spoke, "Nora, I am sure that these young people here would enjoy the city and what it has to offer for a time, but I believe Kate is right. Our community here is very close, and if any of us were to—change in such a—way that you speak of, it would be very difficult for us to find the same comfort we draw from one another here. Your offer is very kind to Kate, and I know that you have only her very best in mind. Please understand that Kate has always desired to remain here, even alone."

Mrs. Morgan's sweet countenance reflected the love she had in her heart for Kate. Kate listened with gratefulness as she so gracefully came to her defense.

Aunt Nora's countenance softened even more. "Well, if she has friends such as you then I suppose she is not alone.

Ah, you are right, my dear. Katherine would never be happy living my life. I suppose I have always been jealous that my sister had the daughter instead of me." She reached over to pat Kate's hand. "I believe your mother would be very proud of your spirit and your love for what they have left you here."

Kate's face had softened as well and she nodded, "Thank you, Aunt Nora, for understanding."

That night found Kate and Nora seated once more by the fire.

"What brought you here, Aunt Nora?" Kate asked sweetly.

Nora glanced her way and sighed, "Truly?"

Kate nodded.

"Katherine—Kate. You were very young when your mother died. I am sorry you did not have the chance to know her better." She gazed into the shimmering coals of the fire. "She was such a woman. Her beauty was reflected in her spirit. There was loveliness in her voice. Her outward beauty was outdone only by her character. Kindness and patience came naturally to her while I fought to keep my strong opinions to myself. Your father saw straight past her sparkling eyes, right into her soul. It was like nothing I had ever seen, their love for each other."

She smiled at Kate, "I watched as each of the dreams we had chattered and giggled about came true in her life. She married the man she loved, and had a beautiful family, a daughter. I began to grow bitter without even being aware of it. One jealousy after another crept up within me. I married my John out of necessity and availability. I had a temper that frightened every other man off."

Aunt Nora laughed and then responded to Kate's look by adding, "Oh, we love each other very much now, mind you. But it did take time."

Kate nodded.

"But on with it. When she died, my jealousies ended. But not just that, I was absorbed in the most unspeakable grief. Grief that I had not loved her more, appreciated her more. I resolved to be like she was, but I have never succeeded."

"I am sure you are like her in many ways," Kate said compassionately.

"I came to your father when she died to see if I could take you and raise you."

Kate's eyes widened.

"You never knew that. He refused and I knew he was right, but I did not like him for it. And so I have stayed away all these years." She paused. "I came back because I had to know what had become of you, if you were like your mother. Now I see that you are her image in beauty and character. I am sorry I did not come sooner. "

The next day Aunt Nora packed up her things and returned to the city, but she left Kate with an invitation to come and stay at her home anytime.

"I know you will never stay there, my dear, but do come for a visit soon."

"You are welcome here any time as well, Aunt Nora. It was very kind of you to come."

"Yes," Aunt Nora said, patting Kate's cheek softly.

Kate thought she saw tears in her eyes. She hugged her tightly before waving goodbye, and found that she was reluctant to see her go.

Chapter V

Mrs. Morgan

One morning when the frost was still glimmering on the window panes, a messenger came from the Morgans'. Kate opened the door to find a farmhand from the Andersons' standing breathless on her porch.

"Can ya come, Miss Kate?"

"Why yes, Jacob. But is all well?" Kate asked, taking her coat and hat from the pegs and slipping her fingers into her gloves.

"Mrs. Morgan, she's awful sick, ma'am."

Kate was alarmed and hurriedly climbed into the wagon that had been brought to convey her the short mile to the other farmhouse.

When Kate reached the home, she was let into the front door and immediately sensed there was something very wrong. Conner sat at the kitchen table, his face in his hands. Weeping could be heard coming from upstairs and Kate knew it was Millie. Her heart sank within her, and she walked silently to the edge of the table. It was a few moments before Conner realized she was there. When he did, he reached up to take her hand. She took his much larger hand in her two delicate ones. She asked no questions, only waited for his explanation, fearing the worst.

"Mother is gone," he finally said, barely above a whisper.

Kate closed her eyes willing it not to be true but knowing very well that it must be. The sobs, the emptiness, the heaviness in the air—all communicated that it must be true. She sank into the empty chair beside him.

"I had no idea she was ill," Kate returned listlessly.

"Yesterday morning she was feeling poorly. But we felt no need to send fifteen miles for a doctor. She insisted that chicken broth and tea would be sufficient." He waited, fighting to get control of his emotions. As he continued, he let the tears run freely down his face.

Kate unconsciously tightened her grip of his hand.

"By the middle of the night, she was so much worse. We sent for the doctor, but I think we—we knew that it was too late." He paused again. "Her last breath was just after we sent for you."

Kate's face was solemn, expressionless. She looked to the stairs.

"Go to Millie," Conner urged.

"But Conner, are you sure that I—"

"She asked for you; she needs you."

Kate climbed slowly up the stairs, bracing herself inwardly for what was taking place. She had no idea how to comfort Millie; her head was still whirling with all that had happened. She did not know what to think. She found Millie sitting on her bed, crying nearly hysterically. Kate sat gently down next to her and slowly put her arms around her. Millie put her face on her shoulder and continued to cry. Kate remained, content to let Millie draw the comfort she needed. Eventually she quieted down. Kate covered her gently with a quilt and walked softly back downstairs.

The house was so still and quiet that Kate was afraid of her own voice. When she reached the kitchen once more, she realized that she still had on her coat and hat and was not uncomfortably warm. She looked around for the reason and there saw the fireplace and the stove, empty and lifeless except for a few struggling coals. Conner remained where Kate had left him. Wasting no time, she crept softly out the door and gathered some wood from the stack close by. She built up the fire in the fireplace and in the stove until they were putting out tangible heat. Conner lifted his head.

"Conner, where's Jess?"

He glanced around the room, "I have not seen her in some time."

"I will be back. I am going to find her."

He nodded.

Jess would be in the barn. She had always found comfort and companionship in the animals. The heavy door slid back on its hinges and Kate walked quietly into the barn and called softly for Jess. There was no answer, but the sound of crying led Kate to the last stall. Jess sat on a pile of hay, her arms wrapped around the farm dog and her face buried in his fur. Kate slipped her arm around her. Jess was startled for a moment, but when she realized it was Kate she flung her arms around her and sobbed. Finally, Kate spoke. She put her hand gently under the girl's damp chin and looked into her eyes.

"Jess, we will all miss her terribly. She was like a mother to you and me both."

The young girl nodded.

"We all need you right now. Can you be strong?"

Jess nodded again.

"Mrs. Morgan will never be forgotten and you will always be taken care of," Kate felt that the young girl needed assurance. When they reached the house, Jess' tears came once again.

"Why don't you go to your room and wash your face and take a moment, and then I will help you with breakfast."

Jess nodded and hurried to the back room.

"Conner, is—is your father—how is he?"

"I should make sure." He rose from the table and moved towards the bedroom. Kate no longer had to endure the clicking of the crutch for he had finally cast it aside. However, her heart ached each time she saw his stiff limp. Now she took a deep breath and went to the row of aprons and tied one around her waist. Even if they were not hungry, she would help Jess have something just in case.

Conner returned shortly. "He's just—in shock. He wants to be alone with her for a bit longer. Jess, please fix Father's cup of coffee and take it to him," Conner requested.

Jess nodded, and looked wide-eyed at Kate at the thought of entering the room where Mrs. Morgan lay.

Kate put her hand on her shoulder and motioned her to the pantry. "Let's get the biscuits started," she said.

"Will you have coffee?" Kate asked Conner cautiously.

He nodded, "I think I will."

She poured his cup and then delivered Mr. Morgan's, tapping softly on the door of his room.

She returned and sat at the table with her own cup in hand, "I could not find the words before," she ventured, "to say how very sorry I am. I could not be more sorry." Kate's guarded emotions struggled to find expression, and she fingered her teacup, endeavoring to find the right words.

He nodded.

The remainder of the day passed quietly. Jess and Kate prepared sandwiches for lunch. By late afternoon, Kate put the barely-eaten food away.

Conner came in from the field. "Looks like snow," he broke the silence.

She followed his gaze to the window and nodded.

"Kate, you don't have to stay."

She looked evenly at him, "I don't want to be underfoot, but if there is a need for me here…"

He smiled, "Then I would like for you to stay."

She nodded.

Just then they heard steps on the stairs and turned to see Millie. Kate went to her side, and Millie clung to her. Kate led her to the table where the three of them sat. Suddenly there was a knock at the door and Kate looked at Conner, puzzled. Who would be calling at such an hour in the snow? Conner rose slowly from the table and went to see who it could be. The girls could not see who the visitor was from where they sat, but they could hear his voice.

"I am sorry to bother you folks at this time, but my name is Williams, Lucas Williams, and I am the new doctor in town. I received word on the way in that a doctor might be needed at the Morgan home. Perhaps you could direct me?"

At the sound of those words, Millie burst into tears once more. Her face went pale and her eyes rolled back in her head. Kate dropped the teacup she was holding and caught Millie. At the sound of the crash, Conner came quickly with their visitor close behind.

The "new doctor" had pulled some smelling salts from his bag and began to administer them. Millie recovered slightly, and they led her to the sofa where they laid her back on a pillow. The doctor spent some time looking into her eyes and checking her pulse. She had recovered more now, although she still looked weak and pale.

"Is there anything particular that might have brought this on, or do you have these episodes frequently?" the doctor asked.

Conner dropped his head and tears formed in Millie's eyes once more.

"Doctor, this is the Morgan home," Kate spoke. "They lost their mother this morning."

The doctor looked horrified, "Oh my, I am so sorry."

"Perhaps she should lie down?" the doctor addressed Kate.

Kate nodded and Millie did not object to being led upstairs to her room.

Kate stayed with her until, for the first time in over thirty hours, she fell off to sleep. When she returned, she was surprised to find the doctor still there. He had spoken at length to Mr. Morgan to assess the cause of death and had administered something to help him rest.

"Will you have some tea, Doctor?" Kate asked, trying to remember to be courteous even in the midst of such tense events.

"No, no, I really must be going." He rose, "It was very nice to meet you, Miss—"

"Oh, Miss Austin; I am sorry. It was nice to meet you also, Doctor Williams. We are grateful for your presence here."

He nodded, both of them painfully aware that his arrival was too late.

"Could you possibly direct me to Doctor Harper's old home? That is where I am to live."

Conner pointed him in the right direction, and Lucas Williams left the warm home for the now snowy roads. Kate hoped he would make it without any problems; their town desperately needed a doctor.

While Millie needed solitude, it was the one thing that Conner dreaded most. Kate fixed more tea and brought him a cup. He did not object and sipped it slowly.

When he looked out the window and realized dusk was quickly falling into darkness, he stood suddenly, "I've nearly forgotten about the animals; Martin has gone to town." He took his coat from the pegs.

"I'll go too." She went for her coat.

"No, no, stay here. You don't have to go."

"Really, I don't mind. It will be finished sooner if I help."

He nodded, and they trudged out into the deepening snow towards the barn. Kate saw that the chicken coop was secure with all its feathered occupants safely locked inside. She added hay to their boxes and gathered the eggs in her apron before shutting the door behind her. While outside was cold and the wind blew in biting gusts, the inside of the barn was warm from the animal heat. She stood in front of one of the horse stalls, gently stroking the muzzle of the big bay.

"Stonewall." She was startled by Conner's voice in the silent barn. "He was born in the middle of the war, just after Stonewall's great stand. Millie named him."

"I remember," Kate said nostalgically.

A glance around the barn provided her with plenty of childhood memories. The hay loft had been a frequent place of games and fun, and the sights and sounds came back to her.

Conner followed her gaze, "Thomas and Caleb and I used to race all the way across the field just to see who could get to the hayloft first. We had some good times up there. You and Millie even joined us from time to time."

She tried to smile, "And if they had come home, they would probably still be running through the creeks, jumping over fences, and riding their horses recklessly."

"They would," he smiled. "No more jumping over fences for me, though."

Kate looked at him suddenly before turning to Stonewall once more, "But you are still the best rider in the county. That hasn't changed."

They pulled the barn doors together and latched them securely. The snow was falling heavily now and complete darkness seemed to engulf the farmhouse. They could see only the one lamp they had left burning on the kitchen table. They took each other's arms and pressed into the wind towards the light, snow crystals hitting harshly against their faces. The door blew open with the help of the wind, and they stepped inside, shaking off the snow. The heaviness of silence and warmth fell upon them. The grief had seemed further away under the expanse of sky, but it met them heavily at the door. Jess had prepared stew and served it. Each tasted it and though it warmed their chilled bodies through, neither could eat more than a couple of spoonfuls.

"Kate, would you mind having tea for the minister and his wife in the morning?" Conner asked, knowing that he could rely on Kate to provide the normalcy that they all needed.

She nodded, "Of course."

She helped Jess and saw that she was tucked into bed. The girl was experiencing her own great portion of sorrow. Kate washed the few used dishes, dried them, and then took the basket of things she had sent for from home. Picking out her knitting needles she absent-mindedly clicked down the rows of the shawl in progress. Her thoughts were elsewhere. Nightfall had deepened the sorrow. It hung so heavily that Kate thought she could almost touch it. She finally laid down her work and lighting a lamp decided she would leave Conner alone. She hesitated as he seemed reluctant for her to go.

"You going to try to sleep?" she asked.

He shook his head.

Kate crept softly up the steps. She would not be able to sleep either, so she stepped quietly to Millie's room and sat in the stuffed chair. She watched her friend's face, still stained with tears, and wondered why so much tragedy had come to this home.

Conner remained downstairs. The solitude enclosed around him and felt as though it would crush him. The door to his mother and father's room had remained closed, his father on the other side with his wife whom all earthly life and color had left. Then it was Kate's face he saw before him; the solemn face with no emotion, no expression. Somewhere buried deep within her was a grief she could not or would not express. A weight was added to his already heavy heart.

The night passed slowly and just as Kate was falling off to sleep, Millie awoke suddenly. Within moments she was nearly hysterical. Kate went to her bedside and held her until she was quiet. Then she slipped into bed beside her and held her hand until they both fell asleep.

Chapter VI

Morning

When the rooster crowed just at dawn, Kate awoke immediately. She slid cautiously from bed so as not to wake Millie and descended the stairs to the kitchen. She was surprised to see the fire roaring in the stove and a fresh box of wood next to it. She looked around the room and was startled to see Conner, his appearance unaltered from the night before, save the dark circles that supported his drooping eyelids. He had not found the same comfort that his sister had in sleep. He turned toward the window as she came in the room and raised his hands to wipe away the tears.

"Oh, Conner, you never slept."

He just shook his head.

Kate made coffee while Jess prepared breakfast, and Millie surprised them by appearing on the stairs. She hugged Kate tightly and then went to her brother. The coffee boiled and the bedroom door opened. Three faces looked up to see Mr. Morgan slowly emerging from his room. He squinted in the morning light that the large windows let in. His hair was disheveled, and if Kate had thought that Conner's eyes were bloodshot, Mr. Morgan's were much more so. He walked to the table and sat. Still no one spoke. Kate set down a steaming mug of coffee just in case he wanted it.

"We should—probably send for—the minister," he finally spoke.

"He is on his way now, Father," Conner replied. His father nodded and rose from the table, taking his coffee mug with him. Millie ran to him, and he embraced her for a moment. Then they listened to his heavy footsteps down the hallway and the opening and closing of the door.

Kate and Jess spent the early hours baking muffins in preparation for the next day and any visitors that might come following the funeral. Millie and Conner remained on the sofa, her head leaning back on his shoulder. Her tears streamed down her cheeks, but she was composed. It was the first time Kate had seen Conner really cry. His tears now spilled over continuously.

They have lost their mother as I have lost mine. But they are much older and knew her much better. How they will miss her. We all will miss her. Their joy must fade now. How could they continue in the same manner without her presence in this home? Kate thought.

The minister arrived, but his wife remained home with the little ones. He flung the reins carelessly over the post and came quickly to the door. He embraced Conner and then immediately asked, "Where's your father?"

Just then, Mr. Morgan appeared from the bedroom once more. The minister met him, and for the first time in his life, Marcus Morgan sobbed uncontrollably on another man's shoulder. Kate took her coat from the pegs, and leaving them with tea and cookies, slipped out the front door. The morning was cold and the fresh snow glistened across the wide open landscape. Kate stared out over the farmland. It bore signs of the war just as her own farm did. The fences were broken down from armies traversing them, but they did not look broken now, not covered in fresh white snow. She went to the barn and stroked Stonewall's warm muzzle. His breath came in clouds, warming her hands.

"Hi, Stonewall," she spoke to him. "You have no troubles, do you?" She waited, almost expecting a reply. He just shoved his muzzle against her. "Where is your mother?" she asked. "I hope you have never missed her."

She stood for a while longer stroking his powerful yet gentle muzzle. She saw the minister come from the house, mount, and ride away, and she started back towards the farmhouse. When she entered the cozy home once more, she found Millie standing at the door to her mother's room.

"Oh, Kate, thank goodness you came back." She rushed to Kate. "We must prepare Mother for the service, and I simply cannot do it alone." Tears were in the poor girl's eyes, and Kate felt pity and horror at the same time.

The color drained from her face, but she managed to sound more confident than she felt, "Then we shall."

They walked together towards the door. Kate braced herself possibly even more than Millie did. The door swung open, and they walked slowly in. Kate heard Conner whisper her name.

"I can do it," she responded without turning around. She followed Millie, and they clung to each other for support as they faced the body for the first time. Mrs. Morgan lay as pale as moonlight. Kate did not realize until then that Conner had followed them and placed a supporting hand on each of their shoulders. Neither of the children had seen their mother since the morning she died, and now the three that stood before her drew strength from one another.

"Are you sure you can do this?" Conner asked them both.

"It must be done," said Kate, gaining her composure though her body was trembling. "We would not want anyone else to do it," she looked at Millie now and she nodded.

Conner left silently, shutting the door behind him.

"Where are the things?" Kate asked objectively. She had avoided emotional breakdowns her entire life by being objective, and she took advantage of that resolve now.

"Yes, here." Millie went to retrieve the white gown and things her mother was to be buried in. The girls worked carefully but quickly, and all in silence. When they finally emerged and shut the door behind them, they jumped at the sound of a human voice.

"You are finished?" Conner questioned.

The girls nodded, but Millie's face flooded with tears. Kate walked to the window and stood staring out. Snow had begun to fall again, but she did not notice. All she could see was Mrs. Morgan's lifeless face. Inside her, a feeling welled up like rage. It was a burning desire to bring to justice whoever had caused this. But there was no one to blame. Amidst all her bitterness, she could not shake her fist at God. She felt Conner's hand on her shoulder, and for a moment she imagined it to be Thomas.

"Kate, are you all right?"

She nodded, but her gaze remained toward the cold, blank snow. Soon it was lunchtime and the smell of Jess' bread served to revive their spirits. It was comforting and familiar. Millie tried to help Kate with the dishes, but Kate refused.

"No, Millie, go sit." Millie obeyed and went to join Conner in the sitting room.

A fresh torrent of tears spilled forth. He put his arm around her, and she cried against his shirt for some time. By the time Kate had finished with the dishes and brought Conner a cup of coffee, Millie had cried herself to sleep once more.

"Conner," Kate suddenly exclaimed, "should we send word to Marie?"

She knew as soon as she uttered the words that it was a mistake, but she remained silent.

"Kate, you know I—have not seen Marie since—since the war ended. Well—I have seen her, in town, twice. But she does not come to church anymore."

"I know," Kate returned. "I can imagine if someone I loved had come home from war—as you did—I would have been scared—no, hesitant and worried. I am sorry; I should not have asked."

Conner studied her expression. Over the last several months, as soon as he could walk, Conner had come by every couple of weeks to make sure that Kate had everything she needed. His company and wise advice on farm matters were always appreciated. Even so, his injury was a painful reminder of the great losses which all had suffered in the war. Some days she had to fight for control of her emotions. Gradually, those feelings began to disappear, and she had been glad to see him, and Millie who often accompanied him, walking up the path to the door. They had bonded in a new way. She unknowingly applied the feelings of sisterly affection that she longed to give her own brothers, to him. Subconsciously, she began to feel towards him the way she had towards Thomas and Caleb. Now, with teacup in hand, she pondered the plight he faced.

"But Kate," he continued, "I do not expect that she still feels that way, that she—loves me still."

"Conner, you don't know that. Give her some time. Perhaps…"

He interrupted her. "Kate. Would you?"

She looked at him a moment, "I would. I would like to believe that I could, and be grateful to have you alive and home. Yes. I am sure of that. I wanted Caleb and Thomas alive and home. That would have been more than enough." In her expression was etched the aches of her heart.

He nodded his head.

Just then there was a knock at the door.

"I'll get it," Kate motioned Conner to stay seated. She opened the door slowly, peering around it to see who the visitor was.

"Oh, hello, Mrs. Simmons."

"Hello, Kate dear. I have heard the sad news from the minister, and I just cannot believe it is true. I judge by the silence, though, that it indeed must be."

"Yes, ma'am, unfortunately it is. Will you come in out of the cold, Mrs. Simmons?"

"Oh no, my dear, thank you, but I just came to bring this." She handed Kate a carefully wrapped cake.

"Marie made it as soon as we heard and insisted I bring it this evening."

"Thank you, Mrs. Simmons; I know the family will be so grateful. Thank Marie as well."

"You're a treasure, Kate. They are blessed to have you here," she patted Kate's cheek and turned to leave.

Kate shut the door behind her and walked the short distance to the sitting room. Conner just smiled. Kate went to the kitchen and set the cake on the counter, peering inside to discover it was pound cake, Conner and Millie's favorite. She would let Conner discover that himself.

"You know she will come tomorrow, Conner," Kate said as she returned to the sitting room.

"Anything now will be from pity," he responded.

"Perhaps the pity will bring out her true feelings."

His expression remained unchanged.

After supper, Kate went to Jess' room; she had not eaten in some time, and Kate took her a small plate. She refused it.

"Jess, you need to eat something." Kate brushed her hair back from her face and saw the tears trickle from her eyes onto the pillow where she lay. "Everything will be fine."

Once Kate made sure that the house was tidy, the baking done, and the dishes washed, she took her coat, hat, and gloves from the peg and set off for home. Conner had offered to accompany her, but she insisted on going alone. She needed the walk. He made her promise she would send word that she had arrived home safely, and she agreed.

"Mrs. Simmons was right; you are a treasure. Thank you, Kate," he said as she left.

By the time she reached the front steps of her own farmhouse, she realized the toll the past two days had taken on her. She was weary—weary from service and weary from grief and sorrow. Anna met her at the door, "Oh, you poor child. Been workin' yourself to death. Always givin' and givin'. You gonna wear yourself out one of these days."

"Oh, Anna, you know how much they have done for me. It was the least I could do." She paused. "I just cannot believe she is gone," she whispered. Anna insisted she get a bath and go to bed early. Tomorrow would be another long day.

Chapter VII

Hidden

Kate rose early, dressed in her best black dress, and pinned her hair up in place. She studied her reflection in the mirror. Her face was pale, and she too had dark circles under her solemn eyes. She tried to eat breakfast, but it got caught in her throat, and she simply could not swallow. The service was to be held at one in the afternoon, so Kate tried to occupy the morning hours. The hands on the clock seemed to move in slow motion. Kate willed the time to pass, and by a quarter after noon, she set off for the graveyard. It would only take a quarter of an hour to get there, but Kate intended to pay a visit to more than one grave. As the snow crunched beneath her feet, she lifted the latch on the little iron gate that blocked free entrance to the graveyard. She went to the back left corner. There stood four tombstones bearing the name Austin. "Thomas Caleb Austin," "Katherine Louise Austin," "Thomas Paul Austin," and finally "William Caleb Austin." Only one Austin waited to join them. Katherine Anne Austin. She stared at her mother's tombstone. Kate herself had been so young; she tried so often to remember what it was like to have her mother around. After all, she had been only six when her mother died, and from six to twenty-four was a long time to remember details. At the sound of the creaking hinges, she turned and found that Doctor Lucas Williams also had arrived.

"You are early as well, I see."

She nodded.

"Are these kin of yours?" he asked, motioning to the graves before her.

"Thomas and Caleb were my brothers, and these two are my parents," she motioned to each tombstone.

Doctor Williams' face was grave. He did not speak or look up at Kate, but simply stared at the markers, as if to let the gravity of what this young girl had just said, sink in. "Is there anyone left?"

"Judd and Anna remained on the farm. I was grateful when they refused to leave after the war…and the funerals," she answered.

More of the townsfolk began to arrive, and Doctor Williams and Kate moved to where the service was to be held. The Morgans came, along with the casket which was borne by several of the men from the town. As the service began, it looked as though the entire town had come out in the cold and snow to pay tribute to Mrs. Morgan, including this new young doctor who had never known her. She had served, comforted, counseled, loved, and prayed for the whole town, and now they had come to give their thanks. Tears flowed freely, and Kate wondered if there would be a new layer of ice surrounding the gravesite. Because of the cold, the minister's message was short, but it gave honor to Mrs. Morgan and the legacy she left behind her. As the casket disappeared beneath the snowline, the neighbors turned to go on their way. Kate saw Marie for the first time. Her face was pale but serene, and her eyes glistened in the cold air. Kate watched as they neared the family to express their condolences.

"I am terribly sorry," Kate heard Marie whisper. But Marie moved quickly on. Conner's eyes met Kate's that were watching him intently, and he made no expression. Kate slipped off to the Morgans' home to see that the tea things were prepared for any guests who might drop by. She also wanted to know what had kept Jess away from the funeral. The family had urged her to go, but she had refused.

"I jest can't stand to see all those people standin' around that casket they set off with. No, I seen enough already." Jess explained.

Kate helped her set out muffins, pound cake, and cookies. The minister and his wife arrived first and were glad to have some hot tea. By the time the last guest left, dusk was rapidly setting in. Kate hastily prepared to go, not wishing to be out in the snow after dark.

"Kate, why don't you just stay tonight?" Conner suggested. "It's nearly dark. I will take you in the wagon if you really want to go."

"No, no, I will be fine; I can walk," she insisted.

But Millie chimed in, "Will you stay Kate? I would like it if you did."

"All right; I will stay," Kate took her coat off. "But you all must want some time alone."

Millie and Conner both shook their heads.

Kate nodded, finally understanding.

Martin went with word to Anna and Judd that Kate would not return home until the next day.

Kate and Millie stayed in the same room that night. Millie needed the company. As they fought for sleep, Millie whispered, "Are you awake?"

"Yes," came the reply.

"Mother loved you so much, Kate."

Kate waited a moment before answering. "She was the closest thing to a mother that I have truly known."

"Oh, my dear Kate, how have you lived all of these years with such strong purpose and resolve?"

"I haven't. Most of the time I feel as though I have no purpose or resolve, just perseverance."

"Oh, but you do," Millie insisted. "I wish we could have had Mother for longer."

"I know you must," Kate replied sincerely. "But I am glad that you have had her for long enough that you will never forget her."

There was silence.

Kate clasped Millie's hand in the dark and Millie spoke, "We will always remember her."

"Yes," Kate whispered. "Always."

Chapter VIII

What Can We Do?

After breakfast and steaming mugs of fresh brewed coffee, Kate and Millie tidied the kitchen for the noon meal. Kate assured Millie that she would come to call in a few days and then took her coat and returned to her own home.

The days slowly passed. The funeral had been on Wednesday and Kate was certain that the Morgans would not be in church. *How could they?* she reasoned. But when she slid into her pew, there they were. Millie even smiled at her. Kate faced the preacher, but she heard little of his sermon.

They have lost their mother and still the joy remains. Kate fought her feelings. For days she struggled with it. What was it that gave them joy in the midst of their grief? Why did they seem so peaceful when Kate knew very well that there was loneliness and sorrow in their hearts? Great deep, sobbing, empty sorrow. She knew it too well.

The next morning she was surprised to see Millie walking up the path. She knocked on the front door, and Kate wondered why. Neither Conner nor Millie ever stopped to knock. Nevertheless, Millie stood waiting outside the door. Anna came from the kitchen, but Kate motioned her to stay; she would answer the door herself. She opened it and stepped aside for Millie to come in. "You knocked," she said.

"Oh, yes, I suppose I did. Well—Conner sent me—or I thought I should—should come make sure you were well. We have not been in a while."

Kate nodded, "Yes. Stay for tea?"

Millie nodded with a smile.

When tea had been served, Kate spoke, "How is everyone, Millie?"

"We are fine." Millie replied in a melancholy tone, but there was the usual smile.

Kate did not answer. Millie watched her closely.

Kate asked all about Conner and their father, if Millie was sure she was doing well, and if she, Kate, could do anything at all. She avoided any talk of herself and by the time tea was over, Millie was rather puzzled. She left and returned home to find Conner studying the paper.

"Well?" he asked, looking up.

Millie hung up her coat and scarf. As she removed her gloves, she answered, "I do not know. She—she seemed so concerned about—us—how we are doing. Of course that is what I expected, I suppose. I kept feeling as though she was keeping the conversation going in such a way that I could not ask her about herself."

Conner nodded as if that is what he had expected.

She looked at him for an answer.

"Millie, do you recall ever seeing Kate laugh or cry since Thomas died?" Thomas had been the last of the three that the war had claimed.

Millie thought for a moment, and then shook her head.

"I think she has hidden her grief all these years, and she does not know how to express it. Or else she just will not allow it. Somehow I think Mother's death has made it even worse. I feel as though she is even avoiding us now."

"Oh, Conner, what can we do?" Millie replied.

"That is the difficult part—nothing. We can go on being there for her just as we have been, but unless she chooses to open her heart, her grief will continue to fester."

"I wish she would come live with us instead of living in that house all alone."

"I believe that is part of it, Millie. She will never leave that place unless she can release her sorrow. Her sorrow is tied to the memories there."

Millie sighed. She ached at the thought that her best friend was hurting and that she could not help. She also knew that Conner protected Kate like a sister and that he too felt the burden of seeing her so sad and being so helpless to assist her.

Chapter IX

Doc

The winter months continued. Kate made new curtains for the sitting room windows, she planned the garden and ordered her seeds, and she began a new quilt. She always visited the sick in the neighborhood and baked bread and pies for those who needed cheering. The weeks passed slowly by, and she remained well occupied. Doctor Williams also stayed busy during the cold months, and Kate was so grateful that when one of the small children in town fell ill, there was a doctor to call for. Unless there was a pressing case to be attended to, Doctor Williams appeared in church on Sunday. Kate admired his tidy appearance. There were many times that she knew he had been nursing a sick child through the night. She had spent a few of those nights with him watching at a little one's bedside. She had a steady hand and a steady mind that he appreciated.

While the town was desperately in need of a doctor, it would be difficult for them to put their trust in one as young as Doctor Williams. Doctor Harper had loved all of the children as if they were his own. Nearly every baby in town had been delivered into his capable hands. He too had come to town as a young doctor, but had won the faithful trust of the people. The town mourned his passing, and it was a struggle for folks to accept a replacement. Nevertheless, Doctor Lucas Williams proved bit by bit that he was well worthy of earning their trust. He was young and robust with thick blonde hair and a naturally happy countenance. He was truly devoted to his profession.

One Saturday afternoon, Kate took to the Andersons' a pot of soup she had just made. She had heard that Martha, the youngest, was sick. With four other children in the family, it would be difficult for Mrs. Anderson to keep up. Kate arrived at the door and knocked softly. Mrs. Anderson herself answered. Kate noticed she looked tired and her hair was hanging loose about her face.

"Oh, Kate, you dear girl. Come inside."

Kate went in carrying her pot of soup. She followed Mrs. Anderson to the kitchen where there was boiling water and poultices in the making.

"Mrs. Anderson, how is Martha?"

"Oh dear, I'm afraid it's the croup."

"And the other children?"

"Poor children, I'm afraid they have been neglected," Mrs. Anderson said as she took the pot from Kate and set it down on the stove.

"Has Doctor Williams been here?" Kate asked.

Mrs. Anderson shook her head.

She led the way to Martha's little bed, and Kate peered down at the pale face. Martha's small body heaved as she tried to breathe normally. She coughed and Kate shuddered. Martha's tiny body protested the constrictions and rattling that shook her. She needed a doctor, but when Doctor Williams had arrived in town, Mrs. Anderson had said she would never trust such a young one.

"Mrs. Anderson, I know you have misgivings about the new doctor," she paused, watching for Mrs. Anderson's reaction. "She needs him."

Mrs. Anderson turned her back and was silent. Suddenly she spoke, "I know, I've been silly not to give him a fair chance. I'll send for him."

Kate stayed at the bedside, smoothing a cloth on Martha's head. When Mrs. Anderson returned, Doctor Williams was following close behind her.

"Miss Austin."

"Doctor."

"Well, now who is this?" Doctor Williams asked lightheartedly.

"This is Martha; Martha this is Doctor Williams. He is going to make your cough better, you understand?"

Martha nodded.

Doctor Williams gently brushed Martha's hair back and listened to her chest. Kate watched his gentle yet capable hands. Once the doctor was finished, he turned towards Kate and Mrs. Anderson and whispered, "I'll need one of you to help. I'm going to give her some ipecac and then apply those onion poultices."

Mrs. Anderson spoke up, "I never could stomach doctoring and such. My other children haven't seen much of me these days, so I'll just go on up to them if you don't mind, Kate. I'd trust you with anything."

"I'd be glad to, Mrs. Anderson," Kate replied kindly, slipping off the coat she still wore.

Doctor Williams and Kate hardly spoke to each other as they concentrated on Martha. It was a long process but finally around midnight, she seemed to have fallen into a somewhat peaceful sleep.

"Well," the doctor said softly, "she should be just fine now."

Kate watched his strong, yet gentle hands as he pulled the soft blanket up under the little girl's chin.

Just like Caleb, the compassionate one, she thought to herself. Caleb had been the taller of the two boys even though he was younger. His broad shoulders and large frame had held a tender heart. When they had gone into town, he would always stop to help the older ladies with their large grocery sacks or toss the ball with the young boys.

Kate came back to the present as the doctor spoke.

"Miss Austin, you were a great help, but I am afraid you must be exhausted. I must get you home or we will be doctoring you next," he smiled.

Kate nodded gratefully and felt for the first time that night just how tired she was. They said goodnight to Mrs. Anderson, and the doctor gave her medicine and instructions for the next few days. "Send for me if you have any concerns at all," he reassured her.

"Thank you," she responded, and Kate saw in her eyes that she was truly grateful.

"You're welcome, Mrs. Anderson."

They stepped out of the house into the cold night, and Kate pulled her coat tighter, shivering in the cold. The doctor had ridden his horse, but he did not mount. Instead he took the reins and walked at the horse's head. Kate followed; she was too tired to protest his escort.

"You must be tired," she finally said. "You've been busy lately."

He smiled, "Most people would be glad to be busy, but I must say busy in my business is not a good thing. I am tired," he conceded.

"Nevertheless, you will appear in your pew tomorrow just as usual, I am sure."

He looked at her.

"I have noticed how you never miss service unless you are on a call. I admire you for that."

"Well, it's not always easy. But I made a commitment when I began practicing medicine that my professional life would never compromise my spiritual one."

Kate nodded. "Still, it is a rest day. We need a healthy doctor." Kate was serious, and she kept her eyes straight ahead.

He studied her expression for a moment before asking, "Miss Austin, what was Doctor Harper like?"

She waited a moment before answering.

"He was the doctor in this town before I was born. There is not anyone here who has not received his kind doctoring. He loved the children, reassured the mothers, and bandaged the farmer's wounds. He was not opposed to going into the slave quarters himself to tend to one of the sick or injured. When he died, something about the town died with him. The people mourned for weeks. It was a difficult time anyway, as the war had just come to a close."

They were quiet for several steps.

"Well, it is no wonder people are reluctant to accept me. That is a tough act to follow."

"You will do fine, I am sure. You already convinced Mrs. Anderson," Kate replied.

When they reached her door, she said goodnight, and he thanked her once again for her help. The doctor turned and mounted his horse.

As he rode away, he wondered at Kate's reserve. *She is so kind and good to those around her, but she seems withdrawn and sad,* he pondered.

Kate went to the window just inside the door and gently pushed back the curtain enough to see the doctor ride away down the lane. He had been very kind.

In all their times together and conversations about life, Kate and Doctor Williams had never discussed their personal lives. Kate realized she really knew very little of him—where he had come from, why he had come, or anything of the sort. Outside of her own Anna and Judd and aside from Conner and Millie, he was the one person whom she saw most lately.

The next morning, Kate slept later than she intended. She ran across the fresh snow that had fallen during her short hours of sleep. It crunched under her boots as she hurried towards the church house. As she entered, the congregation was standing, preparing to sing the first hymn. There was Doctor Williams, just as Kate had predicted, looking alert and put together. Kate scanned the many people that filled the church pews. Many of the empty seats were gradually being filled. While it was healing, it was also difficult to see that the faces were different than the ones that had just recently occupied them. Kate started towards her own pew, but she was startled when she realized that those seats were also filled. She stopped where she was, observing the family that took nearly the entire row. As she forced herself to walk on, she searched for a seat that she could slip into without much notice. Suddenly, she felt a hand reach out and pull her into its row. It was Conner.

"It will be all right, Kate," he whispered.

She looked up at him, her eyes pleading that things really were all right, that Thomas and Caleb and her mother and father's seats would not be forgotten. The Morgans silently shifted down the pew, and Kate slid in. She kept looking at the seats before her, and sadness rose within at the thought that her family's seats were occupied by people who had not even known them.

She wanted to shout it out, "My family sat there! They were good people! They all died, and I do not understand why, but you must know that they were important." Instead, she remained silent and attempted to suppress the bitterness she felt within her. The family was new in town; she had never seen their faces before, and she would have to be friendly. When the service ended, she listened as Mr. Morgan introduced all of them to the new family. They were there from Tennessee and had just purchased a farm on the opposite side of town. Kate breathed a sigh of relief to know that she would not be obliged to call on them as new neighbors. Kate nodded courteously, though she did not feel it, and soon Conner gave her his arm and led her outside.

"Won't you come home for lunch, Kate dear?" Millie asked.

"Oh, you're too kind, Millie, but I am tired. Little Martha Anderson has the croup, and I helped Doc Williams until late last night."

"Then come soon, yes?" Millie asked.

Kate nodded.

"We have the wagon; at least let us take you home," Conner added.

It would be useless to refuse. Conner sensed she was upset.

"Thank you, Conner. I would like that."

"Martha is not in any danger, is she?" Millie asked, as they set off towards Kate's home.

"She is fine now," Kate responded. "And I believe Mrs. Anderson finally has faith in the new doctor."

"That's good," Conner replied. "With all those little ones, she should."

When they stopped in front of Kate's farmhouse, Conner motioned his father to wait and climbed down from the wagon. Kate waited, knowing he had something to say.

"It will take some time to get used to, but you can sit with us now."

Kate tried to look grateful.

"I know," he continued. "It's hard seeing strangers in those seats. I remember when I was fifteen years old staring at the back of Thomas' broad shoulders, wondering when I would ever grow enough to be able to see the preacher again." He smiled, and she looked up at his now tall and broad frame.

There was intense sadness mingled with his smile, "It has not seemed right for those seats to be filled, but now they are. Someday soon, Kate, you'll have a family of your own to fill a pew, and you won't have an empty seat by you anymore."

Kate looked down at the snow scattered at their feet.

"I know," he said again, "you wanted to always remain in those seats."

He put his arm around her and for just a moment, Kate felt secure.

As she stepped back, she looked at him. At least it was comforting to know that he remembered, and he understood.

"Thank you," she said and waved to Millie. "I will come soon," she promised.

Chapter X

Wednesday

Three o'clock, the school bell rang and the children dashed out the door towards home. The dozen or so that lived to the south did not head home, but instead ran towards the Austin farmhouse. It was Wednesday, and Wednesday was the day Kate baked cookies.

It had all begun one Wednesday afternoon during the war, about four years before when Susie and Billy Carter had come by after school to pick up a dress Kate was mending for their mother. She had greeted them at the door with the dress. When she noticed their faces as they smelled the scent of fresh baked cookies, she knew she could not send them away without offering them one. "Would you like to come in and have a cookie?" she had asked.

But Billy had shaken his head, "Mommy says we are not s'posed to dawdle but come straight home. We got chores to do."

Kate had nodded, "Well, how about I bring you a cookie and you can eat it on your way home?"

Susie and Billy had looked at each other. "Well, I s'pose that wouldn't be breakin' a rule. Thank you, Miss Austin!"

The young faces beamed as Kate went to fetch the cookies. They had gobbled them up, and with crumbs still on their faces, taken off towards home. The next week they came on Tuesday and Kate was so sorry to tell them that she did not have any cookies left.

"I do all my baking on Wednesdays," she had told them. "Next week come on Wednesday and I'll have some." They had smiled and nodded and trotted off.

From then on, they always came on Wednesdays and gradually they added a friend or two who walked with them on their way home from school. For years now, every Wednesday all the children who lived south of the schoolhouse could be found after school on Kate's front porch, eating cookies and drinking milk. On this particular Wednesday, Kate was just stacking the last few cookies on the platter. She took it with the pitcher of milk to the front porch where the glasses and napkins were waiting. She did not have to wait long before the happy voices of many children were heard running up the little path. Kate had a strict rule of only one cookie per child; she did not want the parents dissatisfied with her for filling their children full of sugar every week. In truth, the parents appreciated Kate's kindness. She always asked the children about school and their families and challenged their minds with small character lessons.

Just as she was waving to the last little child as he disappeared down the lane, Conner and Millie's wagon appeared.

"Just in time—two cookies left," she held up the tray and they each took one. "Come inside." She motioned her hand for them to follow as she picked up the dishes and headed for the door. "I'll send Anna out for the rest."

They went to the sitting room and Anna brought tea. They talked of the approaching planting season, seeds for the garden, Sunday's sermon, and such until finally Millie said, "Kate, my father and Conner have to go to the city for some business, and they will be gone a few days. Would you mind if I stayed here with you?"

"Oh, of course not. I'd be delighted to have you here, Millie. You know you are always welcome."

"It will be the first time they have been gone—since—since—Mother—I don't think I could bear to be there—alone," she paused. "Kate, I do not know how you have done it all these years."

"You'll be good company for each other," Conner smiled, attempting to lighten the heaviness that had suddenly settled in the little room. Even the sunlight, which had one moment been streaming in, faded as clouds rolled across the sky.

So the next few days found Kate and Millie enjoying each other's constant companionship. Jess had accompanied Millie to help Anna with the first chores of spring cleaning. Anna loved her company as much as her help. It was now late March, and there had been some warmer days. It had been a long winter and they were looking forward to spring. However, when Friday afternoon came, the sky looked threatening and the air was chilling.

"I hope Father and Conner can get home safely tomorrow. The sky looks dark."

Just before dusk, Kate saw someone walking up the lane. It was not one of her normal visitors, and she stood up and went to the window to get a closer look.

"What is it?" Millie asked.

"Someone is coming," Kate said, pulling the curtain back slightly to get a full view of the visitor.

"Oh, it's Doctor Williams. I hope everything is all right." Kate left the room to answer the door.

"Doctor Williams. Is something wrong?"

"Hello, Kate. I just came to make sure that you and Millie have everything you need."

Kate looked surprised, "Oh—yes—yes, we are doing just fine."

"Well, with Conner away, I just thought I'd check in on you," he explained himself. "I hear that there might be a snowstorm brewin'. The sky is looking a little ominous, and there is a chilling wind."

Kate had forgotten her manners in her surprise and still stood holding the door open with one hand while the doctor remained on the front porch.

"Oh my, how rude I am. Will you come in, Doctor? It is cold. I can feel the wind myself."

He stepped inside. "I must be going. Don't want to get stuck in the storm."

"Well, at least have some tea. Have you been out on a call?" Kate asked as she walked towards the kitchen door. "Anna, will you bring another cup, please?"

"Yes, I have." The doctor replied. "Just to make sure that little Martha was doing well."

"And?" Kate asked.

"She's doing just fine—about over the cough completely."

They went to the sitting room where Millie and the doctor greeted one another. As soon as he finished his tea, he rose, "I must go, but if you need anything, please do not hesitate to send for me."

"Thank you, Doctor Williams; your kindness is much appreciated," Kate answered.

"Thank you for coming," Millie added.

When he opened the door to leave, snowflakes were gently falling.

Chapter XI

Snow

That night, the wind picked up and was soon whistling in and out of the shutters and screen doors. Snow drifts rapidly built up against the house. Anna and Judd and Jess had returned to their small cabin, and Kate and Millie struggled to keep the fire built up. Finally, they gave up and hurried upstairs to Kate's room where they climbed in bed together to stay warm. As they snuggled under the double layer of quilts, the cold sheets gradually became warm, and they were soon asleep. The wind and snow continued to blow throughout the night. Millie was awakened once by a loud crash.

Lost a shutter, she thought before falling back asleep.

When they awoke the next morning, the dim sunlight coming through the window indicated that the sky was still heavy with clouds. The room was chilled and the girls were not willing to climb from the bed that held their warmth. At last, Millie counted, "One—two—three!" They jumped from bed and ran towards the pegs, grabbing their dresses and dashing to change.

When they arrived downstairs, they found the fires already roaring, and the stove sizzling with fresh eggs, ham, and fresh-made coffee. Anna and Jess were humming and stacking freshly pressed linens for the table.

"Oh, Anna, thank you!" Kate exclaimed. When she looked outside for the first time, she added, "How did you make it from the cabin in all this snow?"

"Oh, Miss Kate, we just shoveled our way over!"

"Aww, Father and Conner will never make it home in this; they will be stuck for days," Millie said despondently.

Kate looked concerned.

"But that means more time with you, my dear Kate." Millie tried to sound cheerful.

They passed the day in front of the fire reading, sewing, and talking. Neither Kate nor Millie could keep from glancing out the window from time to time as if there was some chance that Conner and Mr. Morgan would attempt the journey home. But the day passed slowly with no sign of anyone. But they were warm, and they were grateful. The snow continued to fall in soft cloudy drifts around the farm. Night fell once again, and Millie sensed Kate's tension.

"You do not think they would try to come home in this, do you?"

"No, Kate, do not worry. They will be wise."

"Of course, I know."

They crawled between the cold sheets once more and were extremely grateful for the hot water bottles Anna had insisted they take with them. Saturday night always brought the anticipation of church, but tonight it was absent. The girls would not be able to make it across the field and down the road to the little church house on the eastern edge of town.

Sunday morning the sun streaming in was bright, and the snow had ceased falling, but it was no warmer, and the snow was more than two feet deep. The girls prepared for a Sunday at home with only each other's company. Judd made sure there was wood stacked at each hearth before returning down the shoveled path to Anna and Jess in their own warm cabin.

Millie and Kate had no trouble building up the fires and had just settled into the sitting room when Millie exclaimed, "Oh my! I cannot believe it!"

"What is it?" Kate asked, following Millie to the window. They went quickly to the door, opening it to let in a snow-covered Doctor Williams.

"Doctor Williams! You must be half frozen!" Millie exclaimed.

He shook off the snow and kicked out the mound that had come through the door with him.

"It must have taken you hours to get here," Kate finally spoke.

"Not quite," the doctor replied.

"You're soaked," she added.

"I was prepared for that," he said, holding up the bag he carried.

Once he was in dry clothes, he returned to them.

"Well," he began, knowing that they would want an explanation. "I figured you ladies would not be venturing out for church this morning."

"No, Doctor, I'm afraid our skirts would not do well in two feet of snow," Millie responded.

"But you could have gone, if you made it all the way here," Kate added.

"Actually, I thought we could have our own right here, if you ladies do not oppose. I received word that the church house is closed due to the snow, and church at home alone just would not do. I spend too many hours alone on my horse to spend a solitary Sunday."

"How kind of you," Millie answered.

Kate nodded.

Kate could not deny that it was a nice little church service they had, and yet she remained her reserved and quiet self. Millie enjoyed it immensely. It felt like something out of a storybook to her. She could just imagine what the fireside scene must have looked like from the snow-covered outdoors.

As the afternoon was growing later, the doctor prepared to leave. But before he could go, there was a knock at the door.

"Hello, Miss Kate." It was Mr. Anderson. "Is Doc here?"

"I'm here, Mr. Anderson. Is something wrong?" The doctor answered, overhearing.

Mr. Anderson motioned him outside.

In a few moments, he returned, "There's been an accident on the road; I'm needed. No, Millie, it's not your father." He responded to her anxious look.

"Bring them here if needed, Doctor," Kate called after him.

The girls kept the fire going, hoping it was nothing serious and wondering if the doctor would return. Dusk was falling when they finally saw two lanterns traveling slowly up the path. They ran to the door and let in three men carrying another man. Rob Miller had no visible wounds, but he was obviously in pain.

"Where shall we take him, Kate?" Doctor Williams asked.

Her parents' room was the only downstairs bedroom, but the crisis of the situation did not provide Kate time to reflect, and immediately, she led the way. She paused only a moment when her hand reached the key, but hearing the groaning of the poor man behind her, she quickly turned the creaky lock and forced the door open.

They laid him on the bed.

"Has someone told his wife?" Kate asked. Rob had just recently been married, and Kate knew that the new Mrs. Miller would be worried.

"I'll go to her," Mr. Anderson volunteered.

"Better walk, John; you see what happens when you try to ride," Doctor Williams called after him.

"Thank you, men. We can manage now," the doctor spoke to the other two, and they followed Mr. Anderson out the door.

"Rob, what were you doing out on the road on a night like tonight?" Kate scolded.

"I'd been stuck in town since—Friday—just—thought maybe—today I could—get home." He talked through his clenched teeth.

"He's broken his leg," the doctor exclaimed.

He gave the two girls instructions as to what he needed and they followed orders quickly. Soon the leg was set and bandaged and Rob was resting, exhausted from the entire event. Kate handed the doctor a cup of coffee as he sat slowly down at the table.

"Accidents do not know the meaning of a day of rest," Kate exclaimed despondently. She remembered how word of her own father's death had come on a Sunday afternoon, just after church. She shuddered.

"Thank you both for your help," the doctor said. By that time it was very late.

Kate was unsure of what to do. It would be perilous for the doctor to attempt the journey home in such drifts so late at night, but where would he stay if he remained?

He solved her dilemma when he spoke, "Kate, if you do not mind, I'd like to remain in the room with Rob tonight, just to make sure he is well."

"Of course, whatever is best," Kate replied.

As the girls took the lamp and made their way upstairs, Millie whispered. "Kate, he is so kind and patient with these catastrophic events that fall so inconveniently before him."

Kate nodded.

Her face was solemn, and as they reached the bedroom, she sat on the edge of the bed. She fumbled with the buttons on her dress and slowly unhooked them.

Millie set the lamp down and Kate spoke, "I can hardly believe I went in so easily."

"In? Where?" Millie asked thoughtlessly.

"All those times when I could not begin to turn the key, and then tonight I hardly stopped to reflect."

Millie had begun to understand, and she sat slowly down beside Kate.

"Oh, Kate, you have not been in the room?"

Kate shook her head. "I suppose it was silly, really. I should have long ago," she paused. "I see now it is in need of a good cleaning after all these months—years."

"No, Kate, it was not silly. Every time I go in my mother's room, my heart aches indescribably."

Kate nodded and the chill of the room began to set in as they hurriedly prepared for bed.

On Monday, Sarah Miller appeared at the farmhouse door; her skirt hung heavy and wet around her ankles. The still deep snow had not hindered her from coming to her husband. She went straight to the bedroom where she wept in his arms. Kate could only imagine the anxiety she must have felt as she waited alone for his return. Rob could not be moved for some time, and so the doctor came a few times to look in on him. It would still be a few days before wagon or sleigh could brave the slushy, slippery roads. Kate and Millie prayed that, for now, no more snow would come. The snow did begin to melt, but slowly.

By Thursday, the roads were dry enough that Rob and Sarah were finally able to return home. The doctor said goodbye to his faithful nurses, and escorted the Millers safely back to their own home.

Kate and Millie now looked anxiously toward the arrival home of Mr. Morgan and Conner. It was not until Saturday around midday when they finally heard the sound of a team and looked out the window to see them having just pulled in. Millie ran out the door to meet them, and Kate stood patiently in the doorway. They came up the stairs to the house.

"Kate, my dear, did you fare all right in the storm?" Mr. Morgan asked, concerned.

Kate nodded.

Conner put his arm around her, "I'm sorry it took us so long."

"Well, I enjoyed having Millie for twice as long," Kate replied.

"Anything dramatic happen while we were away?" Conner questioned.

"Oh, yes," Millie replied. "Doctor Williams came on Friday to make sure we were prepared for the storm and then he came again on Sunday, through two feet of snow, just to have a church service here with us!"

Conner looked at her, surprise showing on his face.

"Oh, but then Rob Miller was thrown off of his horse and broke his leg on the road just beyond Kate's lane. The doctor and some others brought him here. Sarah came on Monday when the snow had finally melted a bit, and they all went home on Thursday.”

“So the doctor and Rob and Sarah were here for all that time?” Mr. Morgan asked.

Conner laughed, “And I suppose they are all spoiled now and will never receive so much taking care of again in their lives.” He glanced towards Kate who had remained silent.

“Glad you are home safely,” Kate said. “We were a tiny bit worried,” she squinted with one eye and looked through the small space she held between her thumb and first finger.

He nodded, “I am glad, too.”

Millie went home that night, and as Kate took the lantern from the table and started up the stairs, she felt the familiar pang of loneliness. The house was so quiet, too quiet. There were no other voices to cheer the halls and rooms. It was only her. Her shoulders sagged under the weight of being alone. Somewhere within her, she felt that she was not entirely alone, but she could not understand it. Perhaps she should accept the offer to live with the Morgans? Or maybe even with Aunt Nora? Just as soon as she had asked the question, the answer, as always, was clear. No, she would not leave her home. She wanted the familiar things around her. She wanted to see the family photo each day as she walked down the hall, to sleep each night under her mother's quilt, and to pour coffee each morning from the same pot that her father and brothers had used before going to the fields. She breathed deeply, trying to remember those days when she would wake to the smell of coffee and the sound of her father whistling. He had whistled frequently and they had become accustomed to it, even comforted by it. One image she could remember was her mother standing there at the stove, scooping up hot biscuits and smothering them with gravy. She insisted it was her job to make the first meal of the day. The other meals were left to Anna.

Kate jerked herself back to reality as she reached her bedroom and set the lamp on the bedside table. She took her flannel nightgown and woolen shawl from the peg. She felt cozy as she slipped it on and then wrapped the shawl around her shoulders. Even though the snow had melted, the nights were still icy cold and Kate hurried to get in bed. As she lay there, attempting to go to sleep, her mind traveled over the last week. The doctor had been so kind. Poor Rob Miller, he had a long road to recovery, and she knew he would be anxious to get back to work. Then she thought of Millie and her family; she was grateful that they were safe and back together. Before she knew it, she had drifted off to sleep.

Chapter XII

Picnic

The snow finally melted and gave way to spring. The winter had seemed long and tedious and so spring was all the more welcome. The first colorful petals appeared along the roadside as bulbs that had long lain dormant began to emerge. Kate breathed the fresh air deeply as she followed Anna down the rows of garden soil. Judd had prepared it and now Anna went in front poking holes. Kate followed, dropping in tiny seeds.

She spoke to the seeds as if they understood, "In just a few weeks, you will show your bright green sprouts and before we know it, our table will be full of fresh fare once more."

Each little spec of life landed softly in the dark soil. It took nearly a week to get all the seeds planted and covered. Now it was time to wait, Kate's least favorite part. Once they had been covered with soil she felt as if they should appear immediately, yielding the fruits of their labor. They would poke their bright green tips through in due course. Her impatience had no impact on the timing of the first sprouts. Until that time, baking cookies, visiting the sick, and cleaning the flower beds would serve to occupy her time. Each Sunday she joined the Morgans just inside the church house and had become comfortable sitting on their row. She had now gotten to know the family who occupied her family's seats. It was still a painful thing for Kate, but like the seeds in her garden, it would take time.

Conner and Millie visited Kate at least once a week and they continued to notice the absence of her laughter. Her face often softened, but her bright smile as they remembered it, was never truly revealed. And no matter how trying the situation or how exhausted she was, her tears never surfaced.

"Perhaps she cries at home, when no one else is around," Millie suggested one night when Conner seemed especially concerned.

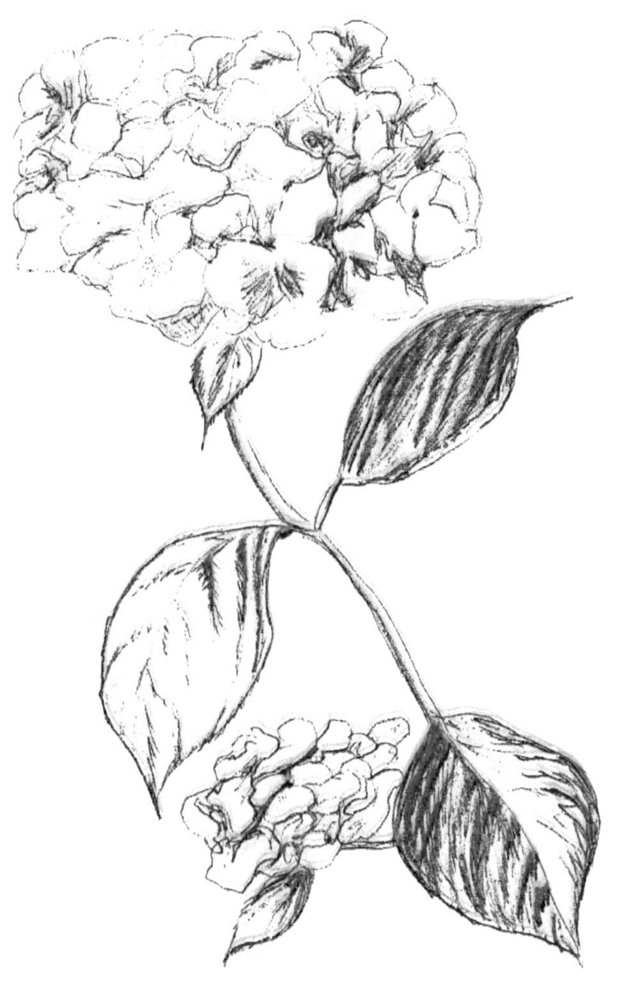

"She blesses so many and everyone loves her. I just know she is hurting in some deep way. There is no way to know until she is ready to talk about it," he replied. "We will wait to see what God uses to heal her broken heart."

Millie nodded and studied her brother. What gave him such vitality since his return home? He had always possessed a generally positive outlook on life, and his injury had not seemed to dampen it. Would she have responded the same way had it happened to her? Trust was a tremendous thing, trusting that God knows best. But her mother had been such a God-fearing woman, why had He taken her? Why had He left the kindhearted Kate Austin with no family of her own? The clock on the wall struck nine times and her eyes felt heavy. Some things she would never understand in this life.

~~~~~~~~

Spring passed and June arrived. Flower blooms were everywhere and Kate's garden had rewarded her by growing heartily. The annual summertime church picnic was in two weeks. It was an enjoyable event that Kate had many fond memories of from her childhood. The Morgans would pick her up and everyone would arrive laden with baskets filled with tasty food.
~~~~~~~~

A few days before the picnic, Kate was at the Carters' assisting the doctor as he set Billy's broken arm. When they finished, it was still light outside, even though the afternoon was late, and Kate insisted that she would enjoy the walk home.

"Well, then," the doctor replied, "will you allow me to escort you to the picnic?"

Kate was surprised. "I am going with the Morgans, but there is no reason why you should not join us."

The doctor nodded, "If you are sure they will not mind."

"Of course not. And do not worry about your lunch; there will be plenty."

Kate walked home under the warm afternoon sun contemplating just what she would make for the picnic. She should talk to Millie about it.

Then her thoughts went to the doctor. She still knew so little of him. What she did know was that he was kind and compassionate. He was not easily flustered, and his face was most often filled by a smile.

Kate called on Millie the next day.

"What are you making for the picnic, Millie?" Kate asked.

"I was going to ask you!"

"Sounds like you girls need to discuss it or we'll end up with an abundance of potato salad," Conner chimed in.

Millie laughed.

"I will fry the chicken; there are more of us."

"Oh, I forgot to say, Doctor Williams asked if he could escort me. I told him he could join the rest of us. I hope that is agreeable to you." She looked from Millie to Conner.

"Of course. He is a nice fellow; I've enjoyed getting to know him better," Conner replied. Something inside of him was disturbed at the thought, though. *Kate should have an escort; that was nice of Lucas. I can't always escort both of the girls.*

"Kate, you make potato salad or something like that, and a sweet. I will fry the chicken, and then—what about those salad greens from your garden?" Millie went on with the menu.

Kate nodded, "They are about ready, and they look delicious."

"Perfect," Millie added. "Jess will make biscuits, and we will bring some of those wonderful sweet onions. I'll make my cream pie to go with your sweet, and that should do it!" Millie exclaimed.

And so it was settled. Kate returned home contemplating her tasks. Finally, Saturday came. She packed her basket with cookies, potato salad, and green salad. Conner and Millie and Jess came in their wagon, and the doctor arrived on his horse.

Mr. Morgan had remained home, "You young people enjoy it," he had said, as he sent Millie and Conner out the door. It was difficult to see their father aging. His wife's death had left him with a sadness that he could not shake.

Anna and Judd also remained at home. Jess ran off towards their cabin, having chosen to remain behind with them.

Kate and Doctor Williams joined Conner and Millie and were a cheerful group as they drove down the dusty dirt road. Kate usually walked the distance between her home and the church house, and now as the landscape moved briskly by, it looked quite different. She could almost see the lines and lines of grey and blue uniforms that had filled the fields, smoke rising from recently fired muskets. She shuddered involuntarily. Blood and death had been so near, even right within her own home. She brought herself back to the present as she heard the doctor speak her name.

When they arrived, there were several families already there. The tables had been set up and colorful quilts and cloths were being spread out across them. Doctor Williams helped Kate down from the wagon and took the basket from her. He was at ease and friendly, and it helped Kate to also feel at ease. It had been a long time since she had been escorted by anyone but Conner. They claimed a table of their own and spread out the quilt Millie had brought with her. Gradually they unpacked the dishes from the baskets they carried. Conner peered over Millie's shoulder trying to see what had caused the tempting smells he had endured for the last two days. The Andersons greeted them warmly and the Carters arrived with Billy bearing the evidence of his broken arm.

"No sack races today, Billy," the doctor said, tousling the boy's hair.

Billy nodded solemnly.

Finally, Pastor Barnes raised his hands, calling for silence and attention. He gave a blessing on all the food and families present, and then happy voices joined together as dishes were passed around and the food was served. Millie's chicken was very good; she had learned from her mother, Kate noted. Soon after lunch, some of the games began. The four watched from their seats as the children joyfully joined in.

As the afternoon wore on, Kate and Doctor Williams went for a stroll. They watched the games as they continued and did not speak for some time.

Finally Kate broke the silence, "Doctor, did you fight in the war?"

He waited a moment before answering, "No," he paused again. "I had just completed my medical training. I remained in my hometown and doctored the armies as they came through."

"Well, you fought in your own way," Kate replied pensively.

He nodded, "I suppose so. At least that is what I told myself. Nearly all of my friends went off in uniform to fight with gunpowder. In many ways—I—suppose I was—glad for a real reason to stay. As a doctor, war seems so— brutal."

"It is brutal, Doctor," Kate said, looking towards Conner as he stood with some of the other young men that had returned from war. There were very few of them that did not bear some evidence of it. The doctor followed her gaze.

"He never complains, does he?" he asked.

Kate shook her head. "Not that I have ever heard. I do not understand it."

He studied her for a moment.

They walked the rest of the way in silence and soon rejoined the others. By the end of the afternoon, they were tired, and when the moon began to rise, they were glad to head home.

Kate deposited the dishes in the kitchen and headed straight for bed. She walked slowly up the stairs, her feet sore from all the events of the day. Conner had felt it as well; he had limped more and more as the day went on and his attempts to conceal his grimaces did not always succeed.

Why is it... she thought once more, *that he never complains? Neither does Millie. And they continue with such joy. Do they not see the hills and valleys covered with army wagons once more? Can they not hear ringing in their ears the ferocious sound of booming cannons? Do they not remember what it was like when Conner first arrived?*

It had been there, in Kate's farmhouse. He had been wounded in a battle that they had listened to all through the night. He was brought in on a stretcher; Kate could not bear the sight of it then, and she squinted now at the memory. It was his mother that retained her presence of mind and along with the surgeon, saved his life and his leg. Kate slipped deeper within the covers, trying to get away from it.

Have they forgotten it all? she wondered to herself. Perhaps that was it. Then she saw the faces of the others who had filled the tables at the picnic. There were happy faces, but many still bore traces of the war. Kate reached for the Bible that lay on her bedside table. She opened it as she had done many nights before and prayed that God would show her the passage that she needed. Lately, the verses had not spoken to her as they once had. She could remember when there was no hardship that could not be overcome by spending a few moments passing through the Psalms. Now she struggled with where to begin. She fingered the pages towards the back and then let the book fall open. She glanced down the pages and let her eyes stop on a verse. It was Romans chapter fifteen, verse four: "For whatsoever things were written aforetime were written for our learning, that we through patience and comfort of the scriptures might have hope."

She looked up from the page and closed the book slowly, "I know," she said out loud. "I know it's true. But Lord, I just don't seem to be able to grasp it these days—

these years. I just don't feel the hope." She thought for a moment. *Just keep seeking. That's what Mrs. Morgan would have said.*

Chapter XIII

The Tree

Sunday's rain showers brought a bright sunny Monday. Sunlight danced back and forth on the wood planked floor beneath the window in the little upstairs bedroom. The crystal clear air, washed from the rain, was sweet from the roses eagerly creeping their way to the split shake roof. Kate finished her household tasks quickly. She wrapped the sandwich Anna had made and tucked it into her flower basket with a cloth and trimmers. The sunshine beckoned her to walk and be warmed and enjoy the colorful bounty of flowers. There was a little woodland path that ran from her farmhouse all the way to the Morgans'. She tied on her bonnet and with the basket over her arm, set out down the path. The sun trickled in through the branches that were thick with green leaves. A robin whistled from a tree branch overhead. Squirrels dashed quickly from tree to tree, carrying nuts and chattering at the forest intruder. Kate walked on, taking in all the sounds and smells. Before she knew it, she was at the edge of the Morgans' land. Many of the children had played in these woods growing up. Kate remembered how well-worn the path had been then, without a stick or a leaf on the hard-packed earth that weaved in and out through the trees. Now the path was covered in leaves, and much less traveled in the recent years. Kate stopped walking, hushing the crunching of leaves beneath her feet, and listened to the birds once more. But this time there was something more than just the chirping of birds and chattering of squirrels. There—a girl crying, sitting at the base of a tree, her face held in her hands, and a basket of flowers beside her. As Kate took another step, it startled the girl, and Kate stopped.

"Marie, are you well?" she asked, placing her own basket on the ground and moving closer to the weeping girl.

Marie dried her eyes quickly.

"Oh, yes, I'm fine," she replied. Kate's eyes traveled from the girl up the tree trunk to the letters engraved there. The date read "1861" and the initials were C.M. and M.S. She looked back with pity at Marie's red eyes.

"I was out picking flowers today—for Mother—and—and I wandered in this direction—and before I knew it—here I was!" Her tears came again.

Kate touched the tree trunk, sliding her fingers over the sunken letters.

"I didn't know this was here," Kate said.

"Oh, it was silly," Marie responded.

Kate slid down to Marie's level.

"I don't think so," Kate said softly.

Marie looked at Kate with surprise, then quickly looked back down, studying the pattern on her skirt.

"Oh, Kate, what has the war done to us all? One minute I think I know who I am and what I'm doing, the next minute I don't have any idea."

Kate nodded. "Marie, do you not think it would help you to talk to him?"

Marie ran her finger across her skirt, following the vine of little roses, and shook her head decidedly.

"You know that he is doing very well?" Kate asked, searching Marie's expressions.

Marie did not respond for some time.

"Perhaps that is just the reason that I cannot bring myself to see him," she replied, her lips quivering with tears threatening once more.

"What about church, Marie? You haven't been back." Kate was bold, and she saw Marie's eyes flash.

"How can you still go, Kate? With all God has taken away from you, and you still go every week to praise Him. I cannot do it. I always find an excuse not to attend with Mother and Father."

Kate had no response. She thought back to the night before when she herself had struggled with the reality of God.

Marie stood up suddenly, glancing at the letters on the tree. "I should be getting back; Mother will wonder if I have fallen in a ditch," she smiled at Kate.

Kate stood as well and nodded. Without another word, Marie walked back towards the path and disappeared. Kate remained where she was. All these years and all those trips down the path and she never knew this little place existed. She studied the letters, wishing they could speak to her of what had taken place the day they had been engraved.

What had they said to one another? she wondered. *I know they were very fond of each other. It must have been just before the war.* Reluctantly, Kate moved on.

Marie was holding a lot of bitterness; bitterness not aimed at those around her, but at God Himself. Kate decided that there was nothing more that she could do except pray for Marie, herself, and all the others who were struggling to find peace and hope after such horrible times.

She continued down the path, filling her basket to overflowing. Suddenly, through the trees she could see the Morgans' farmhouse. She had not intended to call, but she could not come all this way and not pay Millie a visit. She would have to conceal her encounter with Marie; it would only hurt Conner to know, and she was sure that Marie would rather it be kept private. The little gate squeaked as she pushed through, and Millie appeared wiping her hands on a dish towel. "Kate, I'm glad you came!"

Monday was Millie's baking day, and Kate enjoyed a cookie. Conner was in town with his father, so Kate relaxed and talked easily to Millie.

"Millie, have you experienced the presence of God?" Kate asked, peering into her glass.

Millie looked at her and waited a moment before answering.

"Well, most of the time it is not at the time that I feel it, but afterwards that I realize He was there."

Kate nodded. She soon rose to go; she needed to get back and put the flowers in water.

"Thank you for the visit. I was going to call on you, but I was afraid the baking would not be done in time." Millie gave Kate a hug and waved to her as she walked down the path once more.

When Conner came in for supper that evening, he noticed that Millie was thoughtful.

"Have a nice day?"

She nodded. "Kate came by—she…"

He waited for her to go on.

"She asked me if I have experienced the presence of God. I didn't quite know how to answer her."

Conner just nodded, "She's getting closer."

"To what?"

"To finding what it is that has hidden the enjoyment of life that she used to find so easily."

A pleasant summer passed, and autumn arrived with the anticipation of a busy season. As Kate watched the seasons trade, she was fascinated with the changing landscape. The leaves turned, and she often found herself taking tea on the porch wrapped in a shawl, enjoying the colorful display. This year, the cold set in earlier than usual. By Thanksgiving, it was cold enough for snow, and by Christmas, they had nearly a foot on the ground. Kate enjoyed Christmas at the Morgans', but the family and Kate felt an emptiness that no one could fill. Mrs. Morgan's chair was unoccupied and the pain of it all was revisited. The previous Christmas had been Kate's last time with Mrs. Morgan. She could remember vividly how Mrs. Morgan had sat there next to her, gently conversing. Kate remained her solemn self and only once did Conner see the slight smile that had become her only expression of joy.

Millie's grief was probably the most visible as tears formed often in her eyes and her wistful expression made her seem miles away. Jess disappeared just after the meal; she went to the animals in the barn. Millie found her there often in the days following

Mrs. Morgan's death. Mr. Morgan especially felt the sorrow and excused himself early to go to bed. The others remained around the warmth that the large fireplace produced. Millie made tea and with the gift wrappings discarded and the dishes cleaned, the three spent a quiet evening.

Just before they went up to bed, Conner said a prayer. Kate opened her eyes and studied the small room. She looked from Conner to Millie, watching their serene countenances and listening to Conner's words that indicated great trust in his Heavenly Father. She closed her eyes again tightly just as he said amen. Kate and Millie dragged their tired feet up the stairs and hugged at the top before going to their own rooms. Kate climbed in bed and pulled the quilt up under her chin; the room was chilly. She had spent many nights in that room over the years and it had come to be called her own. She kept some of her things there at Millie's insistence and always felt welcome to occupy it. She looked at the lamp still burning on the bedside table, and then she looked towards the ceiling. She shivered, hoping that the covers would soon warm the bed beyond the hot water bottle at her feet. She pulled her arm quickly out from under the quilt and extinguished the lamp before dashing back under the quilt and shivering once more. She peered through the pitch black of the room; slowly it became lighter as her eyes adjusted. The moonlight coming in was especially bright as it reflected off of the snow. She thought about the day and all that it had held.

"I know you are real, God; I know it," she said out loud. "I just don't feel it!" Suddenly she turned over face down and disappeared under the quilt. She was very soon asleep.

~~~~~~~~~

With Christmas past, the new year arrived with a fresh layer of snow. January was bitterly cold, and there were many sick children because of it. Millie and Kate both assisted the doctor as he made his rounds nursing the sick ones. Thankfully, the worst of the weather passed quickly and by Valentine's Day, the infirmary list had diminished.

With the holidays gone and the bleak days of winter set in, the house seemed so quiet to Kate, and she was thankful for Anna's chatter in the kitchen. Even so, the usual empty feeling of loneliness crept in. She fought it, but all her efforts did not amount to enough to prevent it. There was the family portrait in the hall once more. She looked at it, and she felt the burning of her heart within. Anger was beginning to set in and she hardly knew it. She was angry and she did not know at whom. She just knew that she was very sad and very alone, despite the busy days she had and
~~~~~~~~~

the many kind people who surrounded her. She sighed and trudged slowly up the stairs.

Chapter XIV

Peace

One night in February, as Kate was returning from the chicken coop just at dusk, she spotted a horse and buggy coming up the lane.

Why would Conner be coming at this hour?

But as he neared, she realized it was Doctor Williams.

She quickened her pace, hoping it was not an emergency.

"Good evening, Doctor. Nothing is amiss, I hope?" she greeted him as he dismounted.

"Oh no, no, everything is fine." He responded to her look of alarm.

"However, Sarah Miller is having her baby tonight, and I need some help. This is the first baby I have delivered here and your presence of mind seems adequate for the task."

Kate's knees had gone weak at the thought. "Oh, Doctor Williams, I've never done that before. I'm afraid I would not be much help."

"You can boil water, can you not?" he asked with a smile.

She nodded.

"Then you are qualified."

"Well, what about Millie?"

"I saw Millie in town just now, and she was busily occupied with other tasks."

Kate hesitated.

"Miss Austin, babies do not wait on the doctor, you know. I really need to hurry."

Kate realized the urgency of the moment and started quickly for the house.

"Anna, Sarah Miller is having her baby tonight, and I am going to help the doctor. It may be morning before I return."

"Sure thing, Miss Kate. But you be careful, you hear?"

Kate climbed in the doctor's buggy and they set off. The cold February wind stung Kate's face. She had no idea why she had agreed to come along. She had never assisted a birth and the last one she had been present for witnessed both a life and a death.

They arrived, and the doctor went straight to the bedroom. Kate looked around the room as her eyes adjusted to the lamplight. Suddenly she heard groans and cries from the bedroom. She felt her chest tighten and the room began to spin. The doctor returned to find Kate about to collapse. He went to her side and put a strong arm around her. "Miss Austin, are you well?"

No, she was not well, but she did not have the courage to answer. The bedroom was now quiet and the doctor led Kate to the sofa. He sat down next to her, waiting for her to speak.

"My youngest brother Caleb was born on a night much like this." She startled herself for speaking of it. "That night, I witnessed both the coming of a life and the departing of a life." She paused and he remained silent. "My mother died just moments after Caleb was born. I have not been present for a birth since then."

"Oh, Miss Austin, I am terribly sorry. I would not have asked you to come tonight if I had known."

"You had no way of knowing," Kate replied. "I have never spoken of it."

"Would you like to return home?" he asked kindly.

"No, someday I am going to have to face it. I have yet to find peace elsewhere, so I might as well remain."

Doctor Williams stood and went to the window, studying the barren winter landscape. Kate watched him, wondering at his sudden pensive countenance.

"It seems such an injustice for a child to lose a parent, or both parents," he finally broke the silence.

She looked up at him, his face illuminated by the moonlight shining through the window panes, and did not know how to respond. He spoke as though he had felt the pain himself.

"My parents died before I was old enough to know them. When I was twelve years old, a wonderful couple adopted me. I was bitter and sad and confused. I saw people around me in difficult situations, but they seemed content and I wondered how they could be. I came up with all kinds of reasons why they should be happy and I should not. But it never worked. Then my parents—the ones who adopted me—told me that I should stop looking. I was even more confused. I wanted to be happy again and they told me to stop looking. 'Peace,' they said, 'came on a clear night in a stable full of animals to a carpenter and a virgin. There was no royal ceremony, no celebration. Just a stable and a manger full of hay. The Son of God in human form came to earth to live as a human and to experience all the grief and sorrow that we experience ourselves.'" His voice had become nostalgic and it sounded almost as though he was talking to himself. "Finally, he was scorned and mocked and ridiculed and condemned to death on the cross. He died a sinner's death. But the story does not end there." He looked at Kate who had years of tears brimming in her eyes.

"He stayed in the grave only three days and then He rose. He conquered death, He conquered the evil one, and He conquered all the grief and sorrow that we can experience. There is our hope of peace." He came to sit next to her. "You know all that, Miss Austin, I am sure. Forgive my preaching."

But Kate's tears had finally spilled over. All of her pent-up sorrows that she had longed to release, now had no check on them and they flowed freely. He took her in his arms and she wept. He pulled a handkerchief from his pocket and gently dried the tears from her cheeks.

"I have blamed my mother all these years for leaving us like she did. Then—when the rest of my family—died, I think—I think I blamed God for taking away nearly all of my joy in—in life."

He nodded, understanding.

"When Mrs. Morgan—died—I just could not face—her family's peace—anymore." She looked up at his face for the first time and saw that he was listening intently. "I'm sorry, I hardly know you. I've never told that to—to anyone—before."

Noise came from the bedroom once more.

"I need to go," he said. "You going to be all right?"

She nodded.

He started towards the bedroom and she rose to follow.

"I want to help," she said in answer to his questioning look.

"Are you sure?" he asked.

"Yes. The baby won't wait for you to go looking for more help, especially when I am fully qualified."

He smiled. "There should be water boiling in the kitchen. Bring it to the room—and see if you can find some clean towels."

Kate did as she was told and soon found herself with Sarah Miller. The hours passed slowly by as they watched and waited. Finally, just before midnight, the Millers' new son arrived. The doctor handed the tiny baby to his mother, and she snuggled him affectionately.

"Do you have a name, Sarah?" Kate asked.

"Yes, I think so. Matthew—Caleb Miller, and I think we will call him Caleb."

The doctor looked cautiously at Kate, fearing that the name might evoke more painful memories. Instead, he saw, through her tears, a smile spread across her face. "It is a beautiful name," she said, and fresh tears spilled over. "A strong name."

~~~~~~~~~~

Conner and Millie were just about to blow out the lamps and retire to their rooms for the night when Millie spoke. "Oh, I wonder if Sarah Miller has had her baby."

"Was it coming tonight?" Conner asked.

"Yes."

"Did Doc know?"

"Yes, I met him in town this afternoon. He asked me if I could help, but the buggy was filled with things I had to get home and put away. He said Kate was the only other person he knew that would do, and I agreed that she would be a great one to assist."
~~~~~~~~~~

Conner's face turned grave. "He was going to ask Kate?"

Millie nodded.

"Millie, I am not sure that is a good idea. You know that the last birth she was present for…"

Millie gasped. "Oh my, how could I forget? Poor Kate; I am supposed to know her so well, and I did not even think of it! But she will refuse if she feels she can't do it, surely."

Conner went for his coat.

"Where are you going?" Millie asked.

"I'm just going to make sure everything is good."

"Conner, be careful."

~~~~~~~~

The doctor bundled up the tiny baby and handed him to Kate. "His mother needs some rest. Will you take care of Caleb?"

Kate nodded, taking the precious bundle that he offered her. She left the bedroom, closing the door behind her and walked softly towards the lamplight. She studied the baby's tiny features and slipped her finger into his little clenched fist. She was startled by a knock at the door, but before she could get to it, Conner opened it slowly.
~~~~~~~~

"Millie told me, and I saw the doctor's wagon. Is everyone all right?"

"Look, Conner," she said, and she smiled a beautiful smile, a smile that brought one to his own face. He also noticed the tear stains that crinkled up on her cheeks. "Isn't he beautiful?"

He put his arm around her and looked into the sleeping face. "Yes, Kate, he is."

"His name is—Caleb."

Conner looked blankly at her, his face full of sadness. But when she turned her face towards his, she smiled, and her tears fell freely once more. He clasped her free hand in both of his. "Oh, Kate," he whispered.

"I will tell you about it later," she said.

Just then, Doctor Williams came from the bedroom.

"Conner, is all well?"

"Yes, I just came to check on everyone. Millie told me she saw you. "

Lucas nodded, understanding.

Rob Miller also appeared, "I'll take the baby, Miss Austin. You must be tired out. I cannot thank you both enough for being here."

"It was a pleasure, Rob. I will send word to Pastor Barnes, and I am sure that Mrs. Barnes will be by soon. Please tell Sarah to send for me if there is anything you need," Kate responded.

He nodded his thanks.

Conner shook his hand. Rob and Conner had been friends since they were very young and had been in the same company during the war.

"Congratulations, Rob, a son; you must be so proud."

The doctor was putting on his coat.

"You're leaving?" Kate asked.

"Yes, my work here is done for now."

Kate cast a glance towards the closed bedroom door.

"She's sleeping. She is in no danger now, Miss Austin," he put a reassuring hand on her shoulder.

Kate nodded.

They walked out into an even colder night than they had left.

"Kate, why don't you come home to Millie tonight? I know she will be waiting to hear and it is closer than going to your place."

Kate nodded. "Thank you, I will."

"I cannot tell you how much I appreciate your help, Miss Austin. You did a fine job," the doctor spoke.

"I am the one who is grateful to you, Doctor Williams. You have done more than I can ever say."

"It was an honor, Miss Austin. And please, call me Lucas."

Kate smiled again.

"Goodnight," she said, turning to follow Conner.

Chapter XV

Tears

Kate looked up at the sky and was amazed at the expanse of stars.

"Look how beautiful!" she exclaimed.

Conner watched her.

"What are you smiling at?" she asked.

"I see a smiling Kate that I have not seen in quite some time."

"I know," she said softly. "It was such an amazing experience—that," she looked back towards the house. "The joy of a new life with nothing to shadow it." They were silent for a moment as Conner untied the reins.

"I just brought the horse," he realized.

"That is fine; can he handle two?" Kate smiled.

"If you don't mind, I'm sure he won't."

When they reached home, Millie was waiting.

Kate had not prepared herself for what the sight of the home would do to her already fragile soul. Conner reached up to help her down, but she seemed preoccupied.

"Kate?"

Finally, she slid down from the saddle. They walked through the front door and Kate cast a glance around the room. Suddenly before her passed all of the many times she had spent in the farmhouse, surrounded by the family she had come to call her own. The events of the previous year were the last to appear before her mind's eye, and as she recalled them, she was once again brought to tears. She had never shed a tear through the trying days during and following Mrs. Morgan's death. Millie saw her face.

"Oh, Kate, I am so glad you came. I was so worried. Oh, and it took you so long, Conner; I was about to come looking myself. Kate?"

Kate's tears were flowing freely as she looked up at Conner.

He put his arms around her once more and she cried heavily against his thick winter coat that he had not yet removed. He had seen her glance apprehensively around the room and guessed the reason for her tears.

Millie looked at him questioningly.

"Mother," he replied. "Kate never cried."

Millie nodded.

"I'm sorry, I'm so sorry," Kate said amidst her sobs.

"It's all right, Kate; it's all right," Conner assured her.

"I am sorry, oh so sorry."

"Shh, Kate; we know where Mother is."

"It's not that," Kate said, her face still pressed against him and still covered in thick tears.

"Well, whatever it is, Kate, it's not for you to worry so about," he responded, brushing the hair back from her face.

She looked up at him and he nodded. Millie handed her a handkerchief, and they went to the sitting room.

"I discovered something very important tonight." She paused. "I have been—blaming my mother for going away and leaving us—leaving me. When my father—and brothers died—I was angry with God for—for taking away nearly all of my joy," she choked on her words as her tears continued to slide off her smooth skin and onto her skirt.

"Your family has been my—my remaining joy. Each Sunday your smiles would be—the only thing—that made me feel warm inside," she paused, gathering her thoughts.

"When Conner—was wounded—I thought for sure that—that some of your joy would go away," she hurried on. "But it didn't. Finally, when—when your mother died, I thought for sure that you would lose that joy—the joy that she was. When I saw that you were still smiling, I—I withdrew even further." Millie now had streams of tears rolling unheeded onto her own flowered skirt.

"I blamed you for having peace when I could find none. I just held it all inside—until tonight." She stopped to think of her conversation.

"Doctor Williams spoke of the One who has borne our griefs and carried our sorrows, and then I knew that He knows. He knows my grief and your grief," she looked at Conner. "And yours," she looked at Millie. And it is Him—He gives us our peace." They were silent as the reality of the love and sacrifice of their Savior washed over them.

"I can hardly believe I told the heaviness of my heart to a person I know so little about," Kate said, putting her hands over her face.

"Maybe that was just it, Kate." Conner spoke for the first time. "Maybe you needed someone who was there only to listen."

"Kate," it was Millie this time. "We all need reminding of where peace comes from. Do not blame yourself for anything any longer. We are your family, and we love you dearly," Millie squeezed her hand. "Truthfully, Conner and I have ached to know what had caused your reserve these last years. I suppose we knew, but we did not know what to do."

"You did more than anyone could have," Kate hastily replied. "It was my own stubborn bitterness that kept me distant."

Millie put her arms around Kate and hugged her tightly.

"I want you both to know how dearly I love you and how much you mean to me. I cannot express my gratefulness for all the love you have shown."

"We love you, Kate. We loved your family," Conner replied, and Kate nodded.

I still have not heard about Sarah's baby," Millie exclaimed, attempting to lighten the conversation, "All went well?"

"Oh, Millie, you should have seen that baby. So tiny! He has the tiniest little nose I have ever seen."

"And what is his name?" Millie asked anxiously.

Conner reached for Kate's hand as he answered Millie. "Caleb. His name is—Caleb. "

Chapter XVI

Remaining Joy

That night, Kate lay in bed staring at the wooden boards that ran crosswise on the ceiling. There were fifteen rows; she had counted them over and again as she had lain there in that room. How many nights in the years since the war had ended had she wrapped herself in this quilt and snuggled in the warm bedroom of the Morgans' beautiful farmhouse. Even during the war, although she had been persistent about remaining in her own home, she had spent countless nights in that very room, feeling safe and secure. As she studied her surroundings, her thoughts went back to the kindness and love she was surrounded by this evening. She felt so undeserving, and she choked back her rising tears. She saw Millie's understanding eyes and felt the touch of Conner's reassuring hand once more.

Why had she never felt more for Conner than the brotherly love that came so naturally? He had been so kind to her, so understanding, and he seemed to care so much. She searched deep within her heart, wondering what was truly there. But all she found was that same sisterly affection. He had always been as a brother and a friend to her. And then there had always been Marie. Before the war, Kate and Millie had teased Conner about Marie, just as two sisters would. Marie had been so anxious to be with him. When he was around, the light in her eyes would dance. She cried the day he left for the war. But it was when he came home in the middle of war, the one time he was able to visit, that her worry showed the most. She was reluctant to let him go, and she seemed afraid that he would never return. Kate could see it all in her memory, just as clearly as she could see her own father and brothers on each of their last visits home. When Conner returned from war, there was hardship and pain. Marie had not been a part of it, nor did she seem to want to be. Kate remembered her own fear. It was only when she saw his joy that she was able to face him once again in the same way as before. She remembered at the service for Mrs. Morgan how Marie had spoken to Conner for the first time, but Kate had read trepidation in her dull eyes.

They do not sparkle anymore, Kate thought. *I have not been a good friend. I should have been to call on her more often. Perhaps she needs encouragement. She really should come back to church. I will go and visit her soon, maybe even tomorrow, and perhaps Millie will go too.* Suddenly Kate remembered that verse she had discovered weeks before. She reached up for the Bible that always occupied the bedside table. Quickly she fingered the pages.

"Oh, where was that verse?" she said aloud. "I did not take the time to notice the reference."

She knew it must be in the New Testament somewhere and she finally remembered Romans, but as her eyelids began to protest the search, she finally gave it up. Placing the Bible back in its place, she blew out the lamp. "I must find it," she murmured to herself and fell asleep.

The next morning the sun was pouring through the window, and she squinted in the bright light. As she breathed deeply, she was astonished to find that for the first time in many years she was happy to face the day. She pulled on her dress, smoothed her hair back in a ribbon, and quickly descended the stairs to find Millie and Conner already in the kitchen. Mr. Morgan was finishing his coffee. It was a brisk and beautiful morning.

"Good morning!" Kate declared, greeting everyone with her smile they had so dearly missed.

Millie smiled in return, hugging her friend.

Conner said good morning and goodbye as he was headed out the door.

"Well, girls, enjoy the day," Mr. Morgan interjected. "I'm off to town—have some special orders coming in early this morning."

"Is Conner going with you?" Millie asked.

"No, he is going over to the Millers' to help repair a fence."

Kate and Millie sat down to their own tea and breakfast.

Millie was so happy to see Kate's smile present at their table once more. Their prayers had been answered. She also knew that Kate was going to have difficult days, just as she herself did, but the joy and peace in her soul would brace her for the days when despair came creeping back in.

"Millie, I was thinking about something last night."

Millie listened intently.

"Marie has not been to church in some time, and I think maybe I have not been to call on her enough."

Millie nodded, "I have thought the same thing lately."

"I saw Marie recently, by accident really, and I realized that there is something hurting Marie very deeply." She looked intently at Millie, "Millie, do you remember how she adored your brother?"

Millie nodded sadly.

"I think she still loves him," Kate declared.

"You do?" Millie said incredulously. "Oh, Kate, do you really think that? I know she was fond of him, but she was so young."

"Yes, I really do. But something is keeping her from it," she paused, looking far away. "Perhaps it was the same thing that kept my tears from coming." Her gaze came back to Millie, "I think I will call on her today."

Millie nodded.

"Shall I go also?" she questioned.

"You decide what you think is best, Millie, but I would love to have your company."

After breakfast, they wrapped up a loaf of Jess' fresh baked bread and a jar of blueberry jam and stepped out into the clear, crisp day.

They were soon at the door of the Simmons' home. It was the largest house on their side of town and always beautifully kept. The maid answered the door, and they asked to see Marie. They were led to the parlor where they sat waiting for some time.

"I hope this was not a bad time to call." Kate voiced her concern at the delay.

Just then Marie herself appeared, "Kate, Millie, how nice of you to call." She greeted them warmly, but her agitation was visible.

They chatted for some time and then said they should get back.

"Marie, I have not been a good friend; I should have called much more often. Please know you are welcome to call at my house anytime," Kate assured her.

"And the same from me, Marie," Millie added.

Marie looked nervous. "Thank you; you are very kind," she returned.

Millie and Kate stepped outside and breathed deeply. They walked some ways in silence before Kate finally spoke,

"She seemed so fidgety. Poor girl, she could hardly look at you."

"Perhaps I should not have gone," Millie sounded downcast.

"No, my dear, I think you were right to go. You offered her your friendship. You have taken the first step towards renewing your relationship. She has closed herself off from everyone. I do not know how she stands it. I would never have survived if it had not been for the company and encouragement of my friends." Kate smiled.

Millie smiled as well and the girls linked arms. They dropped by the Millers' home on their return. Millie had some fresh bread to leave in the kitchen. Sarah was resting, but she was proud to have Millie see the baby. Kate saw that many other fresh baked goods had already been placed on the table, proof of the kind neighbors they had.

"Your brother is so good to help Rob with the fence. Several of the men in the neighborhood have been working all morning," Sarah said gratefully to Millie. The girls soon left there and traversed the remaining distance to the Morgans' home. Millie served the two of them a late lunch. Afterwards, Kate said she should be getting home.

"Thank you again, Millie. You are a dear, and the kindness and love you have shown means more than words can tell. I love you," she hugged Millie as she spoke.

"Oh, Kate, I will always treasure your steadfast friendship; it has blessed me beyond words these years," Millie replied.

The girls smiled once more, and Kate set out down the woodland path, waving over her shoulder as she passed the barn. The afternoon sun came through the trees, warming Kate's face. Kate held her arms out and spun around looking towards the sky. Her heart felt so free, and she felt warm happiness within her.

"Thank you, Lord," she whispered. "Thank you for bearing our grief, for knowing how we suffer and promising to be with us. Please forgive me for having so little faith, for forgetting who You truly are."

Suddenly, she thought of Marie. "Lord, please show me how to help Marie."

She walked straight ahead and soon she reached the place where she had left the path and discovered Marie. She decided to see if she could find the place again. Somehow maybe she could learn something of what Marie was suffering; she did not know how the spot would help that, but she continued on. Soon she saw the tree with the letters. She was almost surprised that it really existed. She had thought perhaps it was only her imagination that she had discovered a girl there, weeping over her lost love. She studied the letters more closely this time. They were weather worn but still very visible; they had been carved deeply into the tree trunk. She walked around the tree and looked up towards the sky. Suddenly, she heard hoofbeats and was startled to find that Conner was riding towards her. It was too late to retreat so she walked towards the path. Soon he was there before her, and he dismounted.

"Kate, have you been with Millie?"

She nodded, and saw him look past her towards the tree.

"I'm sorry," she began, "I found it by accident not long ago."

She started to go, but he stopped her, "No, Kate, stay. You have always had the freedom to roam these woods; I thought you would have discovered it long ago." He paused.

"Does Millie know about this place?" Kate asked, hoping that it was not so much of a secret after all.

"No," he shook his head. He surprised her by going on, "This was just after the war began," he walked towards the tree, leading his horse, "right after I joined the army. I was walking Marie home—rather the long way. She was pleading with me not to go. When I told her I had to, that I could not stay home, she asked for some way that she could remember those days." He looked at the letters. "We were so young—I was nineteen; she was sixteen. I told her to have faith, that whatever happened, faith would keep us going. She cried and said she wanted something she could see, so we carved this." He looked at Kate and smiled. "It was when I came home to visit that she was most upset. She begged me again not to go back; she said she knew things would never be the same."

"I remember," Kate said.

"When I came home the last time, I never saw her." He paused again. "Well, you know the rest. She was right; things are not the same."

They were silent for several moments. Kate hardly knew what to say.

"Conner, I think—it is not because—she—does not love you that she stays away but because she does."

Conner sat down and stretched out his long legs, leaning back against the tree, "This really is a beautiful spot."

"She has always had such a tender, compassionate heart. Remember how she clung to those orphans that came through on the train that time? And how she used to get so upset when anyone had a cut or scrape?"

He looked at her confused, but nodded.

"She loves you, Conner, and her tender heart cannot reconcile to the fact that you have been hurt in some way." She paused. "I think her hurt goes very deep. I saw her today."

Conner was juggling three pecans he pulled from his pocket.

"Millie and I went to call. Oh, of course, we did not talk about you. It was just a friendly call; we decided we have not been the friends we should have been to her."

He nodded.

"Conner, will you put that down!" she snatched a pecan as he tossed it up. He continued to juggle the remaining two.

"When you visited home that last time, anyone that could have seen the two of you would never have doubted that you truly loved each other."

He finally seemed to get serious, "Kate, we were young. A bit too emotional about the war perhaps." He paused. "Sometimes hardships in life can reveal our true feelings." He finally found the words to express his thoughts.

She looked at him, and there was not a trace of sadness.

"Kate," he began again, "why is it that we have never been more to each other than brother and sister?" He waited a moment before adding, "You do not have to answer if you would rather not."

"I have often wondered it myself," Kate said. "I believe it is because God knew—I needed a brother," she finished rather lamely but managed to smile.

He returned her smile and nodded.

"Well, I should be getting home," Kate took a deep breath and started to go.

"I am sorry I missed you today; Rob had some fence to repair—biggest pecan tree he had fell right across it."

"Yes, we were there earlier. Sarah was very grateful." He smiled.

"Well, come on," he said. "The horse can handle two."

"No, no, I will walk; you do not have to go. I will be fine, really," she assured him.

"Are you sure? You have had a difficult time these last two days. That picture in the hallway…" he left his sentence unfinished.

She looked at him suddenly, her eyes widening. "You have noticed?" she asked.

"That you often look at it?"

She nodded.

He nodded in return.

She sighed, "You know that I have not been in the boys' room since they…" she too left an unfinished sentence. "But I need to do it alone."

"You are certain?"

"Yes. Besides, you have been working all day and Millie will have supper waiting."

He smiled. "Come back soon, Kate," he reached out and squeezed her hand.

"Don't I always?" she smiled. "Thank you," she added more seriously, "for having faith."

He smiled again and nodded as he watched her disappear through the trees.

Chapter XVII

It's Good to Remember

Kate opened the door to her home and stepped inside. Anna came to meet her and took her coat and gloves.

"And how is Miss Miller?" she questioned.

"Oh, Anna, she had the most perfect baby; he is just beautiful. And she is doing so well."

Anna looked surprised at Kate's vivacity.

"I will be back for supper," Kate said as she walked away toward the hallway. Anna watched her go, shaking her head.

Kate walked slowly towards the photograph. She stopped in front of it as usual and studied the faces. A tear slipped out and fell to the floor unbidden, followed by another and another. She continued up the stairs and stopped in front of her brothers' bedroom door. It had not been opened since Thomas' funeral, and Kate had said that she would never go in. Her heart protested the sight of the empty room and all the memories it would bring, but Kate's mind knew that true and complete healing would not come without doing it. The knob creaked loudly as she pushed the door open. Dust swirled in the afternoon sun. She studied the things on the desk—the inkwell and paper, the collection of empty turtle shells, the leather-bound journal. She walked to one of the beds and sat on the edge. Her hand brushed the feather pillow where Caleb had laid his head to sleep in peaceful dreams before the war. Leaning over, she put her face in her hands as the sobs shook her small body. Tears slid between her fingers. She wept, she ached, she asked why. Finally, she dried her eyes and glanced around the room once more. From now on, she would leave the door open. Remembering was a good thing. Thomas and Caleb had been very dear to her and that would never change. Their memories would linger on, and in her heart would forever be the love that they had shared as a family. The laughter that they had experienced together and the things that they had done had helped to shape her into who she was.

She went to her own room and washed her face and straightened her skirt. When suppertime came, she looked almost herself, and Anna barely noticed the trace of tears. After dinner, she went directly to bed. Conner was right; it had been an emotionally trying few days. She took her Bible from the stand and this time she determined to read with a purpose.

"I will read through the New Testament," she said out loud to the silence around her. And so she began. Her eyes soon began to droop, she turned out the light, and for the first time in a very long time, she cried herself to sleep.

~~~~~~~~~~

The next morning Kate awoke feeling rested. While her heart still held grief that was struggling to be released, she still felt what had not been there in many years—a peace that only comes from the Lord. After breakfast, she bundled up and went into town. She needed some things from the mercantile. As she tied her horse, she met Lucas coming from his office.

"Good morning, Kate," he said cheerfully.

Kate returned the greeting

"How are you today?" he asked lightly.

"Very well, thank you. And you?"
~~~~~~~~~~

"I am well, also. I intended to drop in last evening, and I would have had it not been for Ben Allen splitting his head open. I spent half the night trying to get it stitched up properly. His poor wife fainted, and there are no Kate Austins or Millie Morgans to assist on that side of town."

"Oh, I am sorry. Is he all right?"

"Yes, quite all right. What brings you to town today?"

"Just picking up a few things," she motioned towards the building that housed Mr. Morgan's mercantile.

He nodded.

"If there are any such accidents on this side of town, I will be happy to assist," Kate offered.

"If Conner and Millie do not already have possession of you, then I will certainly take you up on that," he replied with a smile on his face.

"Even if they do, they can always spare me," Kate returned. He tipped his hat and she walked on. *That was rather an odd thing to say,* she thought. *Surely he knows that helping the sick ones is always more important than visits.*

~~~~~~~~~~

Throughout the winter, Kate called on Marie every couple of weeks. Marie was an only child. Her parents were
~~~~~~~~~~

well-off and so Marie had enjoyed many of the luxuries that life in their town offered. Kate realized that now Marie surrounded herself with these little pleasures, as well as with friends who enjoyed them. She came to find that Marie's closest friends were from families who did not attend church. They were more interested in shopping, socials, and travel. Kate knew that if this was the means by which Marie was seeking to rid herself of the sorrow she carried, she would never succeed. Marie began to warm up to Kate so that their relationship was nearly what it had been prior to the war. As spring arrived, Marie dropped by to see Kate's garden. Sometimes Millie was there also and the three girls would walk the rows together, looking for the small green shoots that indicated the seeds were coming to life. Marie always seemed more uneasy when Millie was present.

"I wish she did not feel that way," Millie would say later.

It was a beautiful spring. The cherry tree blossoms were full and vibrant and Kate breathed deeply the sweet aroma they gave off. When the spring breeze blew gently through, it sent the white petals fluttering to the ground in great pinkish-white clouds. Kate was very happy. This year's garden would be double the size of last year's, and she looked forward once again to experiencing the delight of seeing the appearance of the little plants and then reaping the benefits they would produce. She often looked across the rolling fields now green in their new grass, and remembered what the farm had looked like when the fields had been high in cotton and wheat. "These fields should be planted again," she said to herself. "I am sure there are many that could use what they would provide. Father would want them to be planted. Yes, next spring, I'll have them planted."

~~~~~~~~~

The time for the spring picnic at the church grounds soon came. Just as the summertime and harvest picnics were a delight, the spring one was also. They were accompanied by Mr. Morgan this time, and he seemed to enjoy the fellowship.

"Kate, Millie, the food is wonderful, as always," he complimented.

"Well, the chicken is a little crispy and the potatoes a little dry…" Conner chimed in.

Kate and Millie both eyed him suspiciously as he took a great bite of a drumstick.

"Conner Morgan, you know better," Kate teased back.
~~~~~~~~~

He laughed. "It is delicious."

Kate saw Marie's mother, Mrs. Simmons. She had on a beautiful gown and carried a parasol trimmed in lace. Kate smiled. It was pretty. Kate got up from the table and walked towards her. "Good afternoon, Mrs. Simmons. You look lovely."

"Oh, Kate dear, thank you!" she exclaimed, almost embarrassed.

"Is Marie well?" Kate asked.

Mrs. Simmons nodded. "I do not know how to thank you for your kindness to her, Kate. Your calls have meant a great deal."

Just then the dancing began, and Lucas was offering her his arm. The fiddle played, and even the children gathered together to joyfully celebrate the tune. Kate saw Conner observing and thought she saw sadness on his face—an emotion he rarely showed. She smiled at him, and he returned it, breaking his brief reverie. Lucas danced with Marie next, and Kate went to stand next to Conner.

"I love this season," Kate exclaimed. "It is so full of new life."

He smiled at her. She had certainly uncovered her vivacity.

Chapter XVIII

Spring

Kate enjoyed each day of the season. She read outside, sewed outside, and spent many hours exploring the woods and fields on the farm. She found patches of wildflowers she had forgotten. Each day brought a new measure of joy, and little by little, the sorrow in her heart began to fade dimmer and dimmer. Tears still came to her eyes when she studied the family photo in the hall or when Conner spoke of times with Thomas and Caleb, but she was grateful for the tears. She was able for the first time to look back and smile at the many fun times they had enjoyed. Often, when she spent the evening at the Morgans', they would reminisce about old times growing up on the two farms. They would laugh and cry and wonder and wish.

Running a farm was a task not often left to a girl Kate's young age. However, Kate met the challenge and worked consistently to ensure that the farm stayed tidy and that all the stock was taken care of. Tending her home brought the most satisfaction. Often, she opened the windows to let in the fresh cool breeze. Placing a pie in the sill to have its aroma fill the kitchen, setting the table for guests, airing the quilts on the clothesline—these tasks brought her great contentment.

One afternoon when the sky was especially blue, Kate set off towards the Simmons'. She had on a lovely pink bonnet that matched the roses on her dress and she could not help smiling as the cool spring breeze blew flower petals across her path. She met the doctor on his way home. He was carrying his familiar black bag, but he too was smiling. *That's a good sign that no one is terribly ill,* Kate thought to herself.

"Good afternoon, Kate," he greeted her.

"Hello, Lucas. Have you ridden far?" she replied.

"Just to the Millers'; baby Caleb is cutting an early tooth and had his mother worried by his fussiness."

Kate smiled. "It is a lovely day."

"As are you. Have you seen Conner and Millie today?" Lucas asked.

Kate was puzzled. She pushed her bonnet back on her head wondering what he meant. She felt her cheeks blush, and she desperately tried to cool them, which only made it worse.

"Not yet; I was on my way to the Simmons'. I will stop to see Millie after."

"Well, Conner will be pleased." He said, as he turned down the walk towards his house. "Have a nice visit!" he waved.

She wondered why he would say that.

She knocked on the Simmons door, recovering her composure. She met Marie on the back veranda where she was drinking lemonade and reading a novel.

"Kate! How well you look! There is color in your cheeks."

Kate blushed again.

"Isn't it just the perfect day?" Kate said, glancing across the landscape and untying her bonnet.

Marie soon began talking about all the places she had been with this friend or that friend. Shopping, flower picking, tea parties. Kate was delighted to hear, but inwardly she cringed. It was all for the pleasure, and Marie had not truly escaped her burden. Kate prayed for wisdom to say the right things.

They talked for some time before Kate declared, "Well, Marie, I have enjoyed our visit, but I really must be getting back." Kate picked up her bonnet and began tying it on. "Perhaps I will see you soon? There is a special program on Sunday."

Immediately Marie's demeanor changed. "I do not know." She stood quickly to her feet and gave Kate a hug saying goodbye.

Kate saw that Marie's face still looked troubled.

Kate pondered all the way to the Morgans' whether or not she should have mentioned church, but she felt that it had not been wrong. *Maybe it will cause Marie to think about it. I do so want her to come back.*

Kate went from the Simmons' to the Morgans' and met Conner coming out of the front door.

"Kate! You look like part of the day. Lovely bonnet." He kissed her on the cheek, and she put her hand on her bonnet once more, wondering why she had worn it.

"Everything all right?" he asked, noticing her face.

"Oh, yes, fine. Are you going somewhere?"

"Just to the barn; I'll be back."

Kate went inside and took her bonnet off and hung it on the pegs. She almost felt like she was at home when she was at the Morgans'. Millie soon appeared.

"Oh, Kate! I was just on my way out. I was going to find you and see if you wanted to walk."

"Yes, I would like to very much."

"Are you all right?" Millie asked.

"Yes, I think so. It has just been rather a confusing day so far."

"Confusing?"

"Oh, it is of no matter. I am just trying to work some things out."

The girls linked arms and walked down the path. Conner waved from the barn and Kate thought of what Lucas had said: *Conner will be pleased.*

Pleased with what? Kate thought.

She told Millie of her conversation with Marie.

~~~~~~~~~

On Friday, Kate once again walked to the Morgans', this time for supper. Every Friday night she was able, she ate dinner with them. It was a reward for the busy days they spent and a nice time of being together. Kate pushed open the wooden gate that was the entrance to the path. It creaked
~~~~~~~~~

on its hinges, a sound so familiar to Kate that she hardly noticed it. She was surprised when she arrived inside to find Lucas there. They greeted one another, and Millie whisked Kate off to the kitchen.

"I told Conner we should have asked you or at least let you know he was coming," Millie whispered. "But he assured me you wouldn't mind."

"Mind what?" Kate asked, perplexed.

"That Doctor Williams is here!" Millie exclaimed.

"Of course I do not mind. It is your house Millie; you can invite whomever you please." Kate smiled.

They soon sat down to supper. They were all good friends, and the conversation flowed easily.

Mr. Morgan asked Lucas all about his practice and how things were going. Then conversation drifted to business at the store. The train had been robbed just outside of town and so Mr. Morgan was behind on stock a little bit.

Conner glanced at Kate, glad that she was safely with them for the night. She gave him a questioning look, and he shook his head as if it was no matter.

"Well, I need to go to the barn," Conner declared, pushing back from the table. "The cow is about to calve and I just want to see that Martin has things under control."

"I'll go with you," Lucas volunteered.

Millie and Kate began clearing the dishes.

"I will leave you young people to your evening. I am glad you are here, Kate; we are always glad to have you."

"Thank you, Mr. Morgan. I'm here so often, I hope I don't intrude."

"Nonsense, Kate. You are part of the family."

Kate smiled.

Conner and Lucas walked to the barn. It was a cool night but very pleasant.

"When are you two going to get married?" Lucas asked almost teasingly.

Conner paused, looking at Lucas' face. "Kate?!" he asked.

"Yes, I mean, you are..." Lucas left his sentence unfinished and Conner laughed.

"Lucas, we practically adopted Kate when her family died. She is like a sister to Millie."

Lucas looked shocked, "So then, if a young man were to—to want to court her, he—would speak to your father?" Lucas asked slowly.

Conner smiled, "It will take my father and me when it comes to Kate, just as it will with Millie."

Lucas nodded.

"But I can put in a good word for you, Doc," Conner smiled, and Lucas' face brightened.

"Thanks, Conner; I would appreciate that," Lucas replied, his face all a smile.

Conner shook his head wondering what had taken him so long to realize that the doctor had discovered Kate's many virtues.

They returned to the house, and the evening passed very pleasantly. Lucas finally said he must be getting home and reluctantly said goodbye. Conner watched him go, searching his own heart once more to make sure that Kate did not occupy more than what Millie did. For the first time, he felt a real sense of possession over Kate. *Could he really let her go?* Lucas was a fine young man and well-qualified to support and cherish Kate. Suddenly, he found himself resisting. *Had he really said he would put in a good word for him?* He looked at Kate standing in the moonlight. *I think perhaps she really does care for him, anyway.* He shrugged off his protectiveness as being the same he felt for Millie.

Chapter XIX

Marie

Kate took fresh bread or pound cake to Lucas every week. She knocked softly on his door wondering if he was home. She called in the evening, knowing he was home from his office in town.

He answered the door, "Kate. Good evening."

"Hello, Lucas. I just came to bring you this." She handed him the basket she was carrying.

He breathed in the sweet smell that was coming from the bread, still warm in the tea towel that was carefully wrapped around it.

"I'm going to have to start walking to town with all these treats in the house."

Kate smiled.

"You are very kind, Kate, to bring this."

"Sometimes I wonder if you don't spend so much time on your patients that you neglect to take care of yourself."

He smiled, "Do you?"

She nodded. "But," she quickly added with a smile, "you are the doctor, and when I was young, I thought the doctor never got sick himself and could solve any problems of his own." She laughed.

Lucas smiled. "I thought the same thing."

"Enjoy the bread," she said, and was gone.

~~~~~~~~~~

Kate waited a whole week before she called on Marie again. She could tell that Marie was a little uneasy the next time. She was quiet as opposed to her usual chatter, and Kate only waited for her to speak. It was a cloudy day in contrast to the last visit and the girls sat in the parlor with tea.

"It looks like it will rain," Kate finally found conversation, but she felt like old Mr. Clarence who sat outside the Sheriff's Office and talked to everyone about the weather.

"I wonder if this is the beginning of the rainy season. I have so enjoyed the clear sunny days."

"Kate, I have been thinking." Kate looked at Marie who sounded serious. "You need to know something."

Kate remained silent, waiting for Marie to continue.
~~~~~~~~~~

"Someone many years ago told me to have faith about something I dreaded very much. They said to trust that whatever happened would be for the best, that I could trust God." In her voice was a hint of anger.

"I lay in bed every night begging God, exercising my faith, trusting that it would turn out fine. I have never wanted anything more in my life," she paused again and Kate saw the longing in her eyes.

"Well, it did not happen. I had faith that it would be fine and it was not. I—have not been to church—because—I…" the tears welled up in her eyes, "could not—go to a place—to worship a God that had let me down in that way. I have been so angry," now the tears began to spill over, but Kate continued to just listen, "so angry—because I had trusted—and—instead of being rewarded, I was—heartbroken." She looked into Kate's eyes for the first time. Marie was crying hard and Kate also had tears spilling out of her blinking eyes.

Kate reached out and put her hand over Marie's.

"Oh, Marie, I am sorry."

Kate let her cry, and after a little while, Marie spoke again.

"I have watched you, Kate. I have watched your joy come back to you, you who lost almost everything. How can you go on? How can you continue to go to church and serve a God who allows such bad things to happen? I will not do it, Kate. I cannot go back."

They were both silent for some time, Kate struggling to find a response. She had no idea that Marie's bitterness ran so deep.

"Marie, I have found over these last few months that the God we are told to have faith in does not just sit in heaven listening to us and deciding whether or not to grant our requests, to reward our faith, or to show us the way; He actually walks with us. He has already borne this grief for you; He bore all of my griefs with me, He weeps with us and laughs with us. He says He will never leave, even when we leave Him."

Marie's tears were silently soaking her hands as they lay in her lap.

"You do not have to carry the weight of the burden— you can lay it at the cross, at His feet, and He will take it. He will give you peace; He will give you joy. And while it is hard to understand why that same God would not reward your faith in the way you trusted He would, He is good enough to show you, in His timing. It is a benefit to us that we trust. His will is going to be done, whether we trust in it or not. It will only bring us the peace and joy we so desperately desire if we lay our burdens and cares and worries and sorrows—at His feet."

"Kate, do you not see? That is exactly what I did. I gave it all. There was nothing I could do, and He did not take it— He was not good, and I will not go back to that kind of trust."

Kate had nothing to say. All her hopes that Marie was coming to realize her spiritual needs had been dashed in a few moments. Marie's heart was not unreachable, but it sure was closed tightly.

Kate mounted her horse and rode home at a quick pace. The visit to the Morgans' would wait; the raindrops were already beginning to fall. She reached the door just as the sky opened up and the rain began to come heavily down. Shutting the door behind her, she leaned against the frame and cried.

The next morning in church, Kate had a difficult time keeping her mind on the sermon. As she sang the familiar words to the hymns, she could not help but think of Marie who sat at home, unwilling to admit her need for Christ. She had been bitterly disappointed, but Kate had not realized the full impact it had had on Marie's relationship with the Lord. Mrs. Simmons was right when she said that Marie's hurt went very deep.

Mr. Morgan had remained at home; he did not like traveling on days that threatened rain, and so Conner, Millie, and Kate drove in the wagon towards Kate's farmhouse. As they pulled down the drive, the rain began to fall, slowly and then very heavily.

"Oh! Come inside," Kate urged them. "You will be soaked if you drive in this."

They did not need much encouragement. Conner drove the team into the barn and loosened the harnesses before joining the girls indoors. They shook the water from their coats and shoes and went to the fireplace.

Kate went to the kitchen and then reappeared. "Anna will have lunch ready soon and there is plenty."

"Oh, we cannot stay; what about Father?" Millie declared.

"Father will be fine," Conner assured her. "You would be drenched to the bone if we went back now," he said, looking out the window at the sky. "It looks like this one will be here for a while, anyway. Besides, I have a taste for some of Anna's cornbread."

Kate just smiled.

Chapter XX

Big News

The rainy season had begun, and it seemed that the sunny days were gone for a long while. Kate tried to enjoy the cloudy days and she busied herself on sewing projects, as well as a new reading list she made for herself. Her mother's piece of linen remained carefully stored; Kate had yet to think of a purpose special enough for it.

Conner and Millie's uncle and aunt were due to come in on the train, and Kate had promised Millie that she would come the day before to help with the baking and preparations. Jess was cleaning and washing and pressing. The whole household was busy preparing for their guests.

On the day she was to help Millie, Kate watched the streams of water run off the roof of her little farmhouse and form new puddles.

Kate put on her coat and her overshoes and took her umbrella from the barrel by the door. She opened the door and stared out into the rain. She took a deep breath and stepped out in it, hurrying down the path towards the Morgans'.

She stepped inside and heard Millie's voice from upstairs, "Be right there, Kate."

Jess was already at work in the kitchen.

"Smells good, Jess. What is it?"

"Blueberry pie, Miss Kate. Millie says it is her uncle's favorite."

"And he hasn't even had yours yet!" Kate hugged the small girl.

Millie and Kate went up to the bedroom and left the cooking with Jess.

By the time the girls had put fresh linens on the bed and fluffed the feathers and dusted and cleaned, the room looked quite adequate for special guests. It was time for dinner so they returned to the kitchen.

"Whew, it smells good in here. You girls are going to spoil Uncle Bill and Aunt Anne," Conner declared.

Jess just grinned.

"You're completely soaked!" Kate declared.

"It is a wet day. How did you manage to stay dry yourself?"

"There is this wonderful little invention called an umbrella," Kate teased. "You should try it sometime."

Conner smiled. He returned shortly, dry, and Millie handed him a tall glass of milk. Kate slid a cake into the oven, and then they all sat down to enjoy a break and the noon meal. Conner started for the rainy outdoors once more, "How can a man leave a kitchen full of these smells to go to the barn?!"

The girls smiled.

"What's this?" He reached for the oven door and Kate slapped his hand away.

"Conner Morgan, you open that door and you are in trouble," she grinned.

"Fine, fine, I will go in suspense. How about a slice after chores?"

"You have to wait until tomorrow," Kate said, making a sad face and pushing him towards the door.

"Well, I am sure it will be worth it," he chuckled as he took his jacket from the peg and walked out towards the barn.

By the end of the afternoon, the pantry was filled with baked goods, the house had received a thorough dusting and cleaning, and the guest room was ready.

Conner came in and washed for supper. "Father has to stay late at the store. A shipment came in that has to be sorted before tomorrow."

"I wish it wasn't so late and we could help him," Millie added.

"Picked up a piece of news in town today, thought you girls might like to hear," Conner said as they dished up their plates. "Big news."

The girls were waiting eagerly, and he enjoyed increasing their suspense as they sat in anticipation.

"Yes, siree, the whole town was abuzz with it." He continued to serve potatoes pretending not to notice their impatience.

Finally, Millie could take it no longer, "Oh, Conner, stop it. Tell us!"

He chuckled. "Marie is engaged to Mitchell Spalding! Who would have guessed it! And a move to the city is planned for just after the wedding."

The girls' faces fell, and Millie glanced at Kate.

"Well, how exciting, I suppose," Millie exclaimed.

"I hope she is very happy," Kate added absent-mindedly.

"So do I, so do I. Well, shall we pray?" Conner reached a hand out for each of the girls.

Kate went home with a heavy heart. Of course, it made sense. Marie had been spending a lot of her time with the Spalding girls, especially after their handsome brother arrived from the city. It should not have been a surprise that Marie had fallen for him.

Conner had seemed so at ease about it. How could he be? He had just told her not long ago about how difficult it had been to go back to war when Marie had begged him to stay.

Calling on Marie would only be proper. Even though she had made very clear to Kate that she was not open to church and things of that nature, Kate was still her friend. The next day she walked towards the Simmons'. Her heart beat quickly as she knocked on the door.

Marie was cordial and soon declared, "Well, I'm sorry I cannot visit for longer, but I really must get into town. I have so much to do in so little time."

"That's why I came, Marie. I just came to say that I am happy for you."

Marie put her hand on Kate's arm.

"Thank you, Kate. That means a great deal to me."

Kate smiled.

"Kate, I know you are wondering, so I will tell you. There was a time when I think I truly loved Conner." She paused, "But I could never marry less than a whole man."

"But—" Kate began.

"I know, you will say that he is, but he will always be crippled."

<div align="center">~~~~~~~~~</div>

As Kate took her hat and hung it on the pegs at home, she wondered at Marie's honesty and thought to herself, *Oh, and I told him that I thought she still loved him!*

Mitchell and Marie were married two weeks later in the white church house. He had to get back to his job in the city, and they were not willing to be parted. His sister and brother were bridesmaid and groomsman, and he had insisted that the wedding be in the local church. The day was clear and warm, Marie was dressed in the latest style bridal gown and veil, and everyone seemed happy. Mrs. Simmons cried, and Caleb Miller cooed and clapped his hands, and Kate and Millie watched silently. Marie did make a beautiful bride.

Conner and Millie and Kate drove home in the evening light. At Kate's farmhouse, Conner climbed down after her and followed her to the door.

"I'm sorry," she said.

"For what?"

"I was wrong."

He still looked puzzled.

"I thought she still loved you."

He smiled and took a deep breath, "Oh, Kate, you are too good," he paused. "There was a time when we did love each other, but it was a puppy love not firmly grounded in reality. It has been quite a while and you must believe me when I say that I wish Marie all the happiness in the world."

Kate looked into his eyes.

"Truly," he added. "You believe me?"

She nodded with a smile.

"Good girl." He brushed her cheek with his hand. "See you soon."

Kate waved to Millie in the wagon and then turned the doorknob and pushed open the door.

Chapter XXI

All You Could Do

Kate spent many hours in her garden to ensure that the weeds would not take over her precious plants. It never ceased to thrill her each time she discovered a new bunch of vegetables draping from the vines and bushes. She lifted a cluster of green beans that was drooping under its own weight. She heard hoofbeats and held up her hand to shield the sun from her eyes and saw that it was Lucas.

"Mornin', Kate."

"Lucas."

He dismounted quickly.

"I've just come from town, and Mr. Morgan asked me to bring this to you."

It was the bag of flour she had left behind on her last trip to the store.

"Oh, thank you; that was kind of you."

They walked towards the house together. She brushed the dirt from her hands and he led his horse along behind them.

Anna looked puzzled as Kate appeared with a sack of flour. Kate handed it off. "Flour, Anna. Lucas brought it from town."

Kate came back from the kitchen with lemonade for the two of them. He did not stay long; he had to make some calls. She waved as he rode back down the lane.

~~~~~~~~~~

Sunday morning the pew in front of Kate was empty. She wondered if the Bartletts were well. It wasn't often that they missed church.

When the service ended, Lucas walked outside with Kate and the Morgans. They stood in the church yard for some time. Sunday fellowship was a welcome part of the week. Suddenly, a horse and rider came thundering at full speed up the road. It was a young boy and he jumped breathless from his horse.

"Doc? Where's Doc?"

"Here, young man," Lucas answered.

"Doc, you got to come." He grabbed the doctor's hand.
~~~~~~~~~~

Kate recognized the boy as one of the Bartletts. His face was anxious, and she could tell he was eager for the doctor to follow him.

"What is it?"

"An accident…my little sister."

"Wait, Lucas; I am coming with you. You will need help," Kate added.

"Take the wagon," Conner offered, indicating his own team.

Without another word, Lucas helped Kate into the wagon and then swung to the driver seat.

The boy was already on his horse, stepping around in agitation. The animal must have sensed the boy's tension.

"Ha!" Lucas commanded the horses to gallop and the wagon lurched forward. Kate held on tightly, one hand gripping the seat, the other on her skirt to hold it against the wind.

They pulled up in front of the house and Mrs. Bartlett ran to meet them, a look of intense worry on her face.

"Mrs. Bartlett, your son came. What is the matter?" Lucas hurriedly asked.

"Adella, the horse threw her. It was her first time, and…"

Mrs. Bartlett turned deathly pale and could not finish her sentence.

"Show us the way, Mrs. Bartlett," Kate said anxiously.

Mrs. Bartlett turned to lead the way. Lucas and Kate followed her to a room with a large bed, in which lay the small Adella, her father next to her, his hands folded and his head bowed.

Kate had guessed that Adella was about seven and her frame was small. What had her little body endured? Adella's face was as pale as death itself, and her body trembled all over.

Her head was gashed open badly and her hair matted in golden curls on the pillow that seemed soaked through. *Is she conscious enough to feel the pain that she must be experiencing?* Kate thought to herself.

Lucas immediately asked for a cloth to press against the bleeding wound. He took Mr. Bartlett's hands and placed them on Adella's head.

"Press firmly," he said. "Hold the wound together." Kate detected his frustration that this had not already been done.

"They sit in our family's pew," Kate thought out loud.

Lucas moved quickly. Grabbing a blanket that lay at the end of the bed, he wrapped it tightly around her. The wound was still seeping blood, and he called for more clean cloths.

"I've got to get her stitched up," Lucas explained. "But she's lost a great amount of blood."

"What do you need?" Kate asked.

Kate had never seen him look so forlorn. Her chest tightened as she realized the gravity of the situation.

Lucas began washing his hands and directing Kate what he would need from his bag.

He asked Mrs. Bartlett to boil water. It seemed like an eternity before everything was ready. Kate wondered if Adella would hold on that long for she had slipped into a coma.

"She needs a hospital," he whispered only loud enough for Kate to hear. "But she would never make it that far."

Lucas cleaned the wound and began to stitch. Kate watched his steady hands. He instructed Kate every five minutes or so to check the little girl's pulse and breathing. Kate herself felt faint more than once, but she knew she must not create another patient for the doctor.

Doctor Williams completed the stitches; it took ten. By the time the wound was closed, her pulse was barely detectable.

"Lucas, it's almost gone," Kate said frantically.

He felt it himself. "It should get stronger now."

But it did not. It fluttered and struggled, and then it was gone. Kate's soul ached. Her eyes blurred, her knees went weak. She fought for control. She watched Lucas' face as he attempted to bring the life back into her. Finally he hung his head and Kate knew. It was an all too familiar feeling, standing at the side of one whose life had just fled. This one was so young, such a child, so innocent. Adella had lost too much blood, and her small body could not recover. Kate shook her head in disbelief. She saw the jaw muscles flinching in Lucas' cheek; he too was struggling to control his emotions.

Finally he spoke, "We must tell them."

He went to the door. Eager faces met their gaze as they slid the door slowly back on its hinges. Lucas did not need to utter a word; his own face spoke more than any words could have told. Kate stood where she was as Mr. and Mrs. Bartlett pushed passed her. Adella's brothers and sister stood staring at Kate as if they did not understand.

"Is she alive?" Samuel finally asked.

Kate could hardly believe that she was the one at whom the question was directed. It was she who must tell this child that he had lost his youngest sister.

She shook her head and the tears on their faces quickly multiplied. Her eyes followed Lucas as he went to the door. He couldn't bear it. Kate went to Becky's side, the twelve-year-old girl that had just lost her only sister.

"Sweetheart, the doctor did everything he could do."

Becky looked up at her, "But it wasn't enough; he couldn't save her," she fled the room leaving Kate aching even more deeply.

"Miss Austin," it was Bennet, the oldest child. "You did everything you could do."

She nodded, grateful for his faith that it was beyond their control.

The family was soon dispersed. Kate went to the kitchen. As she had suspected, the morning's dishes had been neglected. She kept listening for the door to open, wondering if Lucas was even still there. Kate was glad that washing dishes did not require one to see what they were doing for her tears fell fast and her eyes were clouded in grief. Finally, she finished and hung up the towel. The house seemed completely still, as if no life was there at all. Kate went out the door and found Lucas there leaning against the post, staring up at the summer sky. His face was solemn. She stood at the opposite post and remained silent. His deep voice startled her.

"I've never lost a patient."

"Lucas, I'm so sorry."

He suddenly looked at her, "Are you all right?"

She nodded. "Lucas, you did everything you could."

"But what if I didn't?" he asked suddenly. "What if there was something I could have done to save her that I didn't know to do?"

"I was praying before we even arrived here. We both were." She said it almost like a question.

He nodded.

"Then you know that God gave you the strength to do exactly what you did. Nothing more, and nothing less."

He sighed. "We need to go home now and leave them to their grief. We can send Reverend and Mrs. Barnes to them."

She nodded.

They climbed into the wagon, more slowly this time. The evening was touched by a breeze. This time Lucas did not urge the horses; they walked along at their own slow pace. Kate still wore her Sunday dress, though now it was splattered with blood. Nevertheless, the wind teased its folds as they drove. Lucas looked straight ahead. They drove the team to the Morgans' and straight into the barn. Lucas began to loosen the harnesses and Kate led the horses to their stalls. Conner and Millie soon appeared in the doorway.

"Well?" Conner asked.

Lucas shook his head.

Conner looked at Kate, and her tears finally welled up.

"She had gashed her head from a fall off a horse. She was in shock and had lost too much blood. She needed far more than we could give her," Lucas explained as he hung up the harnesses. He led the other horse into its stall and latched the door.

Millie herself was in shock. "You mean—she—died?" she asked in disbelief.

Kate nodded, "We stopped by the parsonage, and Reverend Barnes and his wife will go first thing in the morning."

"Thanks for the team, Conner," Lucas added.

"Sure."

They walked slowly back towards the house; no one was willing to speak. What could be said? Lucas took Kate's hand. Conner inwardly protested. *If he's going to court her, it's only natural.* But the feeling that he should be the one to comfort Kate did not go away.

Millie insisted that they stay for supper, but there was not much conversation around the table.

"I'll have Martin saddle your horse, Doc." Conner spoke.

Kate and Lucas walked together towards her home. Conner stood in the doorway watching them go and was reluctant to let her out of his sight. Conner would never stand in the way of her happiness, and deep down, he knew that Lucas could give her much more than he could. Nevertheless, he could not shake the feeling that he was letting go of something very precious, and he was not sure that he was willing.

When they arrived at Kate's farmhouse, Lucas thanked her again.

She nodded, "Don't let the doubts take over, Lucas."

He quickly took a deep breath. "I will be fine," he nodded as if he was reassuring himself.

"Lucas, you did everything you could; don't forget that," she placed her hand gently on his arm.

He nodded, "Don't worry." He gave her a quick hug and was gone.

She wondered if he truly believed that he had done all he could. He would go home to a home void of sounds or distractions, and she knew the weight of what had just occurred would grow even heavier than it already was. She stood in her own quiet home. She struggled to keep her mind from despairing. She could still see Adella there—her pale, still face. She shook her head, trying to release it. As she lay in bed, she prayed for Lucas and for all the Bartletts. She struggled to fall asleep. When she finally did, she slept restlessly and woke up more than once in a shudder of disbelief at the loss of the little girl.

Chapter XXII

An Empty Place

All the next day, Kate thought of Lucas. She wondered if he had shut himself up. Her heart longed to go to him, but she remained where she was.

Two days later, the funeral service was held for little Adella Bartlett. The sight of her family all dressed in black with constant tears on their faces communicated true sorrow. Lucas was there, looking as though the world had come to an end.

Kate silently watched him. She saw Mr. and Mrs. Bartlett speak to him, shake his hand. Mr. Bartlett patted him on the back. But Lucas' face only shadowed deeper. Afterwards, food was brought to the Bartletts' home and filled the kitchen with its comfort. Just as Kate was leaving the crowds of people that had gathered there to show their love, she felt a hand on her arm. She turned to find Mrs. Bartlett.

"Kate, I have not had a chance to say thank you."

"Oh, it isn't much, Mrs. Bartlett—just some bread and muffins."

"No, Kate, not for the food, although I am very grateful for that as well. Thank you for what you did. You tried your very best. You and the doctor both. If it hadn't been for you and Doctor Williams, Adella would have died, and we would never have known if we could have saved her or not."

Kate looked deeply into Mrs. Bartlett's sincere hazel eyes.

"Oh, Mrs. Bartlett, I only wish I could have done more."

"You did all you could do, Kate."

Kate tried to smile.

"Kate, that night you told the doctor something I have not forgotten. You said that our pew was your family pew. I had no idea!" Mrs. Bartlett paused. "Why did that make you want to save Adella even more?"

Kate took a deep breath and glanced around her.

"If you would rather not answer, I understand."

"No, it isn't that. Mrs. Bartlett," Kate paused briefly and then continued, "I have lived here my entire life. I was born in the farmhouse where I live. My family attended that same church for as long as I can remember, and the pew where your family sits—was where my family always sat."

Mrs. Bartlett's eyes brightened.

"My mother and father and my two brothers and I sat there, but never all together. My mother died in childbirth with my youngest brother. Her seat was vacant but there was a blue bundle that occupied it. Then my father and two brothers were killed in the war."

"Oh, Kate, I am so sorry." Mrs. Bartlett laid a kind hand on Kate's arm.

"I sat in that pew—alone—for many years. Somehow when I was there, it was as if they were still alive. I could imagine that I heard them singing hymns with the rest of us, I could feel their hands in mine as we prayed, and I could hear my mother whisper in my ear."

"And then we came. Oh, Kate, we had no idea; it was an empty row. I am so sorry. You should have…"

Kate interrupted her. "Mrs. Bartlett, all is well. I have sat behind you now for some time. I have watched your family occupy those seats in the same way my family did.

You sing together, hold hands; your voices carry the love you have for one another." Kate paused as the tears filled Mrs. Bartlett's eyes, obscuring their color.

"That is why I did not want another seat left vacant. I am sorry now that it is." Kate's own tears had broken free from their restraint.

Mrs. Bartlett put her arms around her and hugged her tightly. "That seat will someday be filled again. Bennett will bring home a wife and the seat will be occupied by a new shining face," Mrs. Bartlett caught tears as they spilled out again.

"Please let me know if there is anything you need in the days and weeks to come, Mrs. Bartlett."

Mrs. Bartlett nodded, squeezing Kate's hands.

Kate went in search of Lucas. She needed to know that he was all right. She finally found him, untying his horse from the hitching post, about to mount.

"Lucas," she called.

He turned to see her. "Kate."

She smiled.

He turned the reins over in his hands as he held them. "Why Adella, Kate? Why could it not have been one of the elderly people who had lived a full life?"

Kate listened quietly.

"Why one so young and innocent?"

"Why Mrs. Morgan? Why Katherine Austin? Why Caleb and Thomas?" Kate continued. "How are we to know?" She put both her hands over his, and he looked at her intently. "At least Adella had a doctor, a good doctor."

That night as Kate studied her Bible passage for the night, she tried once again to find that verse she had longed to rediscover, "Verse four, it was verse four," she suddenly voiced.

She turned the pages quickly from Luke to Romans, and beginning in chapter one she read verse four of every one. She forced her eyes to stay open as she searched the Book. Finally, when she reached the fifteenth chapter, she sat up straighter, placing her finger on the verse, and she read aloud, "For whatsoever things were written aforetime were written for our learning, that we through patience and comfort of the scriptures might have hope." She paused, looking up from the page, "'That we might have hope,'" she repeated. "Thank you, Lord," she whispered.

Chapter XXIII

A Wonderful Man

The days and weeks passed. Kate saw Lucas frequently, and gradually, his demeanor began to change. The sparkle in his eyes came back, and his step regained the sprightliness of before. However, their relationship remained the same. Kate had wondered how quickly it would progress from being just a friendship to meaning more. But she began to find that her feelings stayed the same, and she felt no more for him than she had when he had first escorted her to the summer picnic.

The leaves began to change. Hot tea became more precious, books more sought after, fires warmer, and walks more pleasant.

Millie and Kate stood in the kitchen going over their favorite recipes for the holidays.

"I think there is another box of these. I left them in the cellar," Millie went off in search.

Kate walked to the window and looked out towards the barn. There was Conner. He hoisted a bag of feed over his shoulder, bracing himself against the barn. For the first time, Kate realized how strong he was. He had learned to compensate with his upper body strength, and his muscles rippled beneath his shirt.

A whole man, she heard Marie say. He returned for another bag of feed. *He could not be any more of a whole man. A wonderful man.* Suddenly she felt the color rise in her cheeks. *What have I been doing?* she thought to herself. *Here I thought that Marie still loved him, and I tried to encourage her that way. I have told myself all along that we are like brother and sister. But after all, we are not!* Kate took a deep breath. Her feelings had shocked her, and she did not quite know what to do.

"Found it!" Millie called, and Kate brought her thoughts back to the kitchen and the recipes that lay untouched on the counter. Her heart continued to beat fast, and she knew her face was flushed. Millie did not seem to notice and was busy sorting the cards into main dishes, vegetables and sides, and desserts. Kate had no idea how she managed to have input into what their favorites were, but as she started for home, there was a neat little stack to go through later in preparation for the Thanksgiving meal.

As she walked home, she thought over the afternoon. She finally knew where her heart belonged. Did he return her love? She did not know. "Oh, how shall I tell Lucas?" she said to the forest around her. Lucas had truly become a dear friend to Kate, but now it was evident to her that they would be nothing more. She wondered if Lucas felt the same way.

~~~~~~~~~

Millie and Jess came to help Kate and Anna with their canning. The vegetables from the garden had all been harvested and now it was time to put them up for the winter. It took two full days to complete, as pots and jars covered the kitchen. Kate had not seen Conner since that day at the Morgans', and she found herself missing his presence. Before, it had seemed like they were always together, but now Kate felt the separation. In the years past, Conner and Mr. Morgan had come for supper the night the canning was completed. This year would be no different, and it gave them something to look forward to at the end of the day. Lucas had been invited as well, as he had become a part of
~~~~~~~~~

their events on the farm. As the final lid popped closed and the last jar was set on the shelf for use during the months ahead, everyone breathed a sigh of relief.

"Your garden is next, Millie!" Kate declared joyfully.

The kitchen smelled delightful with the roast cooking in the oven, and Anna soon had fresh rolls baking as well. As soon as the meal was sufficiently prepared, Anna and Jess slipped off to the cabin. Anna counted her time with Jess special. She said she reminded her of her own daughters whom she had not seen for nearly three years. Conner was early, and Kate heard him whistling as he came to the door. He stopped to tousle Duke's ears and soon appeared in the kitchen.

He whistled again, "Look at all those jars!"

The girls smiled.

"Looks like a good turnout, Kate."

"The garden did very well. I am pleased."

He nodded, "Hey, what do we have here?" A fresh chocolate pie sat in the window sill. "There must be a spoon covered in chocolate somewhere." Kate handed him a wooden spoon that was coated in chocolate pudding. He sat down at the table, and Kate could not help but giggle.

Conner looked up at her and suddenly noticed how well she looked. Her cheeks were rosy and her eyes all lit up.

The others soon arrived, and supper was served. Kate was nervous. Lucas would be there and he would pay attention to her, and yet she knew that she must tell him soon that it would never work for the two of them to be together. She tried to avoid it by spending time in the kitchen checking on this or that.

Finally, Conner followed her, "You need help in here? You keep disappearing."

She shook her head. "No, Anna will be back to do the dishes. She and Jess went to the cabin for a while."

He nodded, "That was nice. I think Jess has missed her."

Kate nodded.

"Hey, your cheeks are flushed," he sounded concerned. "You are not coming down with something, are you?"

He put his hand to her forehead, and Kate remained silent. Her eyes closed and she could not pry them open for fear of catching his glance. His closeness was affecting her as it had never before.

"It is just from being in this hot kitchen all day peering into pots of boiling water," she tried to sound carefree.

"I suppose so," he laughed, dropping his hand and stepping back.

Does he feel it, too? she wondered.

When they returned to the table, it had been vacated, and they found Mr. Morgan alone in the sitting room.

"Millie and Lucas are on the porch," he declared.

"Did you have enough pie?" Kate asked kindly. "There is certainly plenty more."

"Oh, yes, my dear. I am quite satisfied."

Conner chuckled. His father had already had two pieces.

Millie and Lucas were in deep conversation when they joined them.

"When shall we start your canning, Millie?" Kate asked.

"Oh, probably next Tuesday. We will get all the fruits and vegetables in over the weekend and be ready by then."

Kate nodded.

Lucas soon said goodnight and started off towards home. The Morgans' remained until their eyelids began to droop. They sat on the porch in the cool evening breeze, and were content just to be in each other's company. Finally, Mr. Morgan said it was time to leave.

"It is always nice, Kate. Thank you for the pie."

~~~~~~~~~

Now that her canning was completed, Kate turned her attention back to the usual tasks. She was running low on sugar so she made a trip to town. As she passed the doctor's house, he too was headed in that direction. They walked along together and after their greeting to one another, they were silent. Kate was too occupied with how to speak her heart to notice that Lucas also seemed to have something on his mind.

"Kate." He startled her. "I need to tell you something."

She waited for him to go on. How could she tell him that she did not love him in the way he wanted?

"I have grown to respect you and admire you in so many ways. You have been a great friend to me since my first arrival here in town. I will always be glad for that."

Kate nodded, but she dreaded what was to come.

Finally, he stopped and turned towards her, "But, Kate, I believe your heart belongs to another." He smiled. "Am I right?"

Kate smiled in return and nodded, relief flooding her mind.
~~~~~~~~~

"I am sorry, Lucas. I only just recently discovered it myself."

"Oh, I suppose I have seen it all along," he added. "Just was not certain until now."

"Really?" she asked surprised.

He nodded again.

They resumed their walk, and both seemed to have a weight lifted. Kate noticed their steps quickened.

Lucas spoke again, "Conner is a great man, Kate. He was willing to step aside for me, probably because he thinks you need someone without…" he paused.

"I understand," Kate saved him the struggle to go on.

"Truth is, Kate, I am the one who feels inadequate around Conner."

Kate looked at him, "Lucas, you are a great man yourself. Our community is privileged to have you here. You have become a great friend to so many of us."

He just smiled in return.

~~~~~~~~~

It was Friday of the next week before Millie was ready to start canning. Saturday morning the kitchen was filled with steam as the large pots boiled. Can after can was set on
~~~~~~~~~

the counter to cool before being stored in the cellar. It was a warm day, and they made a pitcher of lemonade.

"Would you take some to Father and Conner?" Millie asked Kate.

Kate agreed and carried the pitcher to the barn. She poured them each a glass. They drank it quickly and had a second one.

"How is it coming?" Conner asked.

"Very well!" Kate said joyfully. "We are down to the tomatoes. That is always my favorite part. Something about the piles of red juicy tomatoes just makes me happy," she smiled.

Conner smiled at her joy. "Lucas will be here soon," he added.

"Well, supper should be right on time!"

Conner watched after her until he heard his father's deep voice.

"Son, when are you going to come to realize that girl was made for you?"

He looked at his father and returned to the harness he was mending.

"Are you going to let our young doctor sweep her off her feet while she is in love with you?"

"Is she? I do not know. He is much more worthy of her."

"Conner, do you love Kate?"

Conner looked his father in the eye. "Much more than I have ever thought I could love someone."

"Then perhaps it is about time you told her," his father replied. "You owe her that much."

Conner sighed. "Do I? I desperately do not want to hurt her. I will see how she is with Lucas tonight."

His father just nodded. Mr. Morgan knew deep down that all Kate needed was to be told.

The evening was pleasant. It had been a long day, but the fact that all the canning was completed was a great reward. Lucas left, and Conner was surprised when he did not offer to walk Kate home. He was frustrated with Lucas for his lack of concern and then reminded himself that he would have begrudged Lucas the privilege if he had offered. Kate soon took her coat from the pegs and started off. Conner walked with her to the edge of the woods where the path began. Anna had gone home earlier to get supper for Judd.

"Thanks for coming," Conner said. "Millie loves it when you are here. And you are so good to Jess." He smiled

"You know I would not miss it." She responded with a smile.

The sun was beginning to set, casting its hue of colors across the land. Conner and Kate stared across the rolling hills of the farm as they changed shades in the light. Shafts of orange and purple shot out from the clouds.

"This land is beautiful. It appears even lovelier than before, having seen it so torn. For the first time in so many years I can look at it without seeing lines of soldiers and wagons, cannons being hauled behind, rows of white tents, smoke rising from the fires. I used to lie in bed at night and think I could hear the gunfire once more. It would make me shudder." Kate looked out across the land.

Conner put his arm around her as she spoke, and she leaned into him.

"And you and Thomas and Caleb and so many others were right in the midst of it all. When the house filled with wounded men, I imagined that life would never be the same." She looked up at him for a moment. "How could so much decimation come to a land?" Kate passed her hand over her face.

Conner had never heard her speak so, and he watched her. Her gaze remained on the horizon as if she could see it all painted in the clouds.

"But, Kate, you were so strong."

She looked up at him again. "No. I was not." She paused. "I was frightened, oh so frightened. Little by little my fears became realities, and all I had to hang on to was stripped from my grasp. I went on, mourning my existence. Only did the ever-pressing needs around me prevent me from dwelling always on the sorrow. As the war ended, and soldiers, weary from years of war, came straggling home, only then did I slowly begin to realize that it was not everything I had lost; only some things very dear to my heart." Her voice became softer as tears came to her eyes. "This land remains, and the people, who have survived the years past, live to tell the stories of the great men who fought here."

He felt the touch of her hand on his.

"Now we stand on the brink of a new generation that, by God's grace, will not be shadowed by war but lifted by the hope that we have for the future."

He nodded solemnly.

The tone of her voice changed, "For the first time in my life I am not afraid of tomorrow. I feel happiness each day when the sun rises, instead of dreading the tragedy that the day might bring." She looked up at him and smiled, and he tightened his hold of her.

She took a deep breath, "I should go. It will be dark soon, and Anna will be expecting me before sunset."

He nodded, "You will be back soon?"

"Yes."

The truth was, she would have been happy to remain just where she was.

Chapter XXIV

That We Might

Have Hope

Every year when canning was completed, Kate thought that things would be less busy on the farm. But it never seemed to happen that way. Conner was occupied seeing the fields harvested, so it was a few weeks before Kate saw the Morgans again. Finally, she made her way down the forest path. As the farmhouse came into sight, Kate spotted Millie and Lucas walking through the field. Millie waved from the distance, and Kate continued to the house. She hung her coat on the pegs and looked around. The house was neat and there were two teacups on the table. Jess was wandering around the kitchen.

"Jess, who's having tea?"

"Oh, jest Miss Millie and that purty man."

"Jess! You mean the doctor?"

"Yes, that's who I mean. He's come to call for three days in a row now."

"Where is Conner?" Kate asked quickly.

"In the barn I 'spect."

Kate grabbed her coat and hurried off in that direction. She had no intention of being the third party when Millie and Lucas returned. This was obviously a courting call, and there was tea for two, and only two. They were still in the field, and it was evident by their slow progress that they were not walking very fast. She slipped into the barn door without being noticed.

She was unaware of the real hurry she had been in until she pulled the barn door shut and stopped to catch her breath. She could hear her heavy breathing now in the silence.

Conner came from the tack room, "Kate, everything all right?"

"Oh, yes, my goodness! I had no idea."

"About what?" he asked as he slung the big western saddle across the stall door and began rubbing it clean.

"There is tea for two in the kitchen, Conner."

"Oh, yes, that. Well, seems it has been going on longer than I realized. It appears that Doc has transferred his affection rather suddenly."

Kate sensed a touch of disapproval in his voice.

She walked to the stall next to him where Stonewall was munching his feed.

"You do not approve?" Kate asked. The horse walked over to the door, and she stroked him as she waited for an answer.

Conner polished the saddle harder. "But Kate, he was courting you. He would never say the reason why he was not anymore, only that you had decided it was not best. Then suddenly he comes along and asks to call on Millie."

Now it was clear why Conner would be frustrated; he thought she would be hurt.

"Conner, we decided weeks ago that it would never work between us."

He stopped, "You did? But you never said."

She shook her head.

"Kate, has he hurt you in some way?" He studied her face.

"No, no. It was not that. I approve of the match for Millie. He is a wonderful man. It was just that—I realized—I…" she turned her back on him.

"That you what?" he asked kindly, putting down the cloth and walking towards her.

"I cannot explain it," she said, putting her face in her hands.

He put his hands on her shoulders and turned her around to face him.

"Kate," he took her hand in both of his and studied it. "Kate, you have never been afraid to talk to me."

She remained silent, looking towards the barn floor.

"Kate," he said softly.

"What?" she asked, looking into his eyes for the first time.

He finally spoke the words he had felt in his heart, "I love you."

A smile spread across her face, "I love you too. With all of my heart," her heart tingled at the words.

"Do you, Kate? Because, Kate, I am not the same. If things had been different, I would have told you long ago."

She smiled. "You are right; you are not the same—you are—much better than I have ever imagined for myself."

He reached out and took both of her hands pulling her into his embrace. "Oh, Kate, what has taken us so long?"

"All good things take time," she smiled and then buried her face against his coat as she had done more than once over the last year. This time there were no tears, and her happiness was the only thing that spilled over.

"Now you know, Kate, why you had to believe that I was happy for Marie."

She stepped back to look at him, and he touched her face.

"Because I have known for a long time that it was you that I loved, a love firmly grounded in reality."

She hugged him again.

"But I had given up hoping this could be," he said against her hair. "Then one night I was reading and I came across this verse. It said: 'Whatsoever things were written aforetime were written for our learning that we through patience and comfort of the scriptures might have hope.' And I thought, maybe, just maybe, God was trying to tell me something."

She pushed back from him and happiness shone in her eyes.

She reached into the pocket of her dress and pulled out a folded card. The fold was worn and the corners frayed. He studied her expression as she handed it to him. As he carefully opened it, he saw those very same words.

"You too?"

She nodded. "I came across it just before that night that Caleb Miller was born. I think God was preparing my heart for the hope that I was to discover."

He put his arms around her again.

"You have been a great part of that hope, Conner. I love you so dearly, so very much."

"Is this what you could not explain?" he asked.

She nodded against his coat. Stonewall nuzzled them, and they laughed. Kate reached her hand out to stroke him. "Yes, I think Lucas knew before I did…that my heart belonged to someone else."

She felt Conner's arms tighten around her.

Chapter XXV

Home

That spring, Katherine Anne Austin and Conner Marcus Morgan were married in the little white town church with flowers tied in ribbons over the doorway. A perfect fit for Kate, her mother's dress flowed with new lace added by Aunt Nora. A garland of pale pink roses adorned Kate's head. Marcus Morgan gave the bride away, only to gain her at last as his true daughter. It seemed the entire town attended, bearing gifts for this happy occasion between these two beloved families.

~~~~~~~~~

Now if you visit Montcrest, you will see the fields are once again planted with crops. Everywhere you look is evidence of a well-managed farm.

When you enter the small white farmhouse, you will notice a carved wood frame. In it is the piece of linen that Kate had saved for a special purpose. Embroidered are the
~~~~~~~~~

words, "Whatsoever things were written aforetime were written for our learning, that we through patience and comfort of the scriptures might have hope. Romans 15:4 "

The End